T. BELL

Letters of Grace

Parts of this book were originally published on Kindle Vella.

Cover: Ya'll That Graphic

First edition

This book was professionally typeset on Reedsy.
Find out more at reedsy.com

To my husband, who will always be my definition of love.

Contents

Prologue

Brooks,

   We were six the first time you asked me to marry you. I said yes in front of the whole first-grade class, and you gave me a Strawberry Ring Pop to seal the deal. I had some stipulations, though. One, you had to ask my dad, and two, our wedding would be on a rainy day. My mom has always loved romantic movies, so I blame her for all my ideas about love and marriage.

   You didn't mind my antics. You just smiled that smile of yours—the one that makes my heart skip a few beats—and said I could have anything I wanted.

   I wonder if it's always been that way—me setting stipulations and you readily agreeing to them.

   I hate thinking of it like that. It makes our life together sound one-sided. I hope you know I would have given you anything you asked. I wanted your dreams to come true too. You just never asked. So maybe it is more one-sided than I think, but I never wanted it to be. At six years old, I knew I would love you—even if I didn't exactly understand what love meant at the time. I'm scared that I still don't know what it means.

   When you asked my dad if you could marry me, I'd never seen a boy more determined than you. Most boys at that age would have been scared of him. To a six-year-old, he loomed as high as the sky. Even now, he is intimidating to most grown men. You didn't let any of that dissuade you.

1

Since that day, I've thought a lot about how you walked up to him without hesitation, and I wonder where that confident boy has gone now that you are a man. You seem lost, and I don't know where to begin to help you find yourself again.

I can picture the confidence you had walking as you strolled up to him, shoulders squared. I think every Southern boy learns to ask for a girl's hand from birth, or maybe you saw it on television, like me, because you stood toe to toe with him and said, "Hey, Mister, I would like to marry Emryn on the playground. I even traded for a Ring Pop at lunch today so she can have a ring. It cost me my favorite rock, but she was worth it. Do you think that would be okay with you?"

Dad's eyebrows shot up in surprise. He looked down at this six-year-old boy standing before him, with shoulders squared, chin lifted in confidence, and a dimple on his cheek. Dad pursed his lips, letting the silence sit for a moment, and gave you his best answer. He told you that if you promised to protect my heart, he didn't see any reason you couldn't marry me since you were out your favorite rock and all. That memory makes me smile, but it also makes me sad. We haven't done a good job of protecting each other's hearts.

A week later, the news station finally called for rain. I planned everything. I laid out my prettiest dress and handed out my hand-drawn invitations to my classmates. But—the next morning, there was not a cloud in sight. Tears made my eyes burn. That was my first real experience with disappointment. Despite my dismay, I put on my dress and said a quick prayer.

Growing up, Dad read the bible to me every night, and I remember him saying something about asking and you shall receive. At the time, he said I didn't quite understand when I asked if that meant I would get the dollhouse I wanted, but I figured it didn't hurt to try with the rain. I got down on my knees and prayed with all my might. All I knew was I wanted rain, and God was the only one who could control the weather.

Mom always said that rain on your wedding day is good luck. It rained on her wedding, and she and Dad have the perfect marriage. Maybe that's where everything went wrong for us. Perhaps we should have waited for the rain that day.

By the time recess rolled around, it still hadn't rained. It was too late to cancel. The whole first-grade class had invitations. We were all meeting under the slide.

You were already waiting for me there, a big grin on your face. It lifted my spirits a little, but you noticed my sadness. You used to always notice my sadness. When did that change? When did you stop seeing me?

That day, as we stood on the playground, your brow scrunched in concentration as you studied my face and asked me what was wrong. I felt silly for being sad. I was probably the only girl in the world who wanted it to rain on their wedding day.

When I told you I was sad about the rain, that grin spread further across your face as if my plight wasn't a concern. You grabbed my hand and pulled me across the playground, yelling across your shoulder for the others to follow. We stopped on the other side by the fence.

I didn't understand what we were doing, but even at six years old, I knew I could trust you. I felt silly waiting for rain when there was not a cloud in sight, but the way you held my hand gently in yours, I would have stayed there forever.

Then, suddenly, the sprinklers turned on across the fence, spraying water droplets over us.

I shrieked as the first blast of water sprayed over me. My cheeks ached from the breadth of my smile as I watched the water arc across the fence and shower down on us. I turned back to you, and you were already staring at me. I knew that day that you would be something special to me for the rest of my life.

People say that life occurs in different stages. I believe this is true for love as well. At any given second, we all have a different definition of love.

My first definition of love was a strong-willed, confident little boy, a strawberry Ring Pop, and a sprinkler. It was simple, but all the best definitions of love are. As I've grown, my definition changed, growing more mature and complicated, but one part has always stayed the same: Brooks Montgomery, you have always been a part of every single one.

Love,
  Emryn

Chapter 1

Emryn

I'm a window. That sums up my current life experience.

I. AM. A. WINDOW.

You know that saying, "You make a better door than a window?"
Well, I am the window.

Unheard. Unseen. Looked through.

That's my current definition of love. I have been standing in my
kitchen for the last ten minutes talking to my husband, only for him to
look through me, failing to acknowledge my existence. He will deny
having this conversation with me one week from today.

"Brooks." I twirl the edge of my hair, hoping he notices. I cut it a
week ago, and he has yet to notice. I won't point this out to him. It's a
drastic change. I cut off over eight inches. I *need* him to notice because
if he doesn't, I'm not sure what that means for our marriage.

That seems silly, even to me, to think that eight inches could mean
the end of a marriage, but it's not just the hair. It's everything about
our relationship anymore. Our communication is minimal. We have it
down to a science: I start a conversation, he ignores the conversation,
and then one week later, he denies ever having it. I get angry for feeling
unheard, and we start fighting.

Lather, rinse, repeat.

It's a cycle of our marriage. One I never saw coming based upon all

5

my other definitions of love I've had with this man.

He's morphed into someone I don't recognize in the past six months—short-tempered, rarely home, and even when he is, he's always on the phone. It's like someone flipped a switch, and the man I knew is gone. I've tried to talk to him about it, but that would mean he deems it fit to be active in our conversation—or at least acknowledge that I am in the same room.

I want to scream and yell and throw things until he sees me—really sees me. But what kind of example would that set for our three-year-old daughter? What kind of example are we setting anyway? I worry that she will look at our lifeless marriage one day and think this is normal. I'm afraid that we are going to be *her* definition of love.

With that fear fresh in my mind, I try again—this time about something more mundane. Maybe if I can get him to look at me, he will notice how I feel like he's slipping away faster than I can hold on.

"Brooks, we need to talk about the schedule next week. I have some things coming up for the party, and you'll have to pitch in a little more."

He doesn't look up from his phone, mumbling some indiscernible agreement under his breath.

I take a minute to stare at this stranger I'm married to. He's handsome. He always has been. His light blue eyes are a shocking contrast to the dark eyelashes framing them. The scruff on his jaw does nothing to hide the strong jawline and muscle there. He runs one hand through his hair, rumpling it. He looks so much like my husband, but I haven't seen the man I married in a long time.

I can tell you the moment I let myself recognize that my marriage was failing. That seems strange to say, as it was such a random moment, one of no true significance, but I remember looking at the clock and thinking that sometimes the moments we perceive as insignificant turn out to be the ones that change our lives.

It was 5:15 p.m., a time that used to be my favorite time of day. I used to rush to the door when I heard Brook's truck pull into the driveway. I could never wait a second more than I had to to hear about his day and tell him about mine. He would sweep me up in his arms, and I would kiss him like he had been gone for days instead of hours.

That day six months ago, I heard him pull into the drive, and instead of rushing to meet him, I felt annoyed. As a stay-at-home mom, I spent all day juggling our daughter's needs, cleaning, and planning an anniversary party for my parents. I had just got off the phone with the printing company working on the invitations for my parent's Ruby anniversary when Brooks walked into the kitchen. I couldn't explain my annoyance until he walked in, not bothering to take off his boots. Dirt crumbled off them onto the floor from whatever construction site he had tromped on that day. He didn't acknowledge the dirt or the clean floors he was dragging it across. He was tense and silent and matched my mood perfectly. I knew something was bothering him, but I didn't want to know. I couldn't bring myself to bring his burden on my shoulders too, so I let it go, at least for the moment. But – then the mood continued. He was snappy and rude. I hoped it was a bad day for both of us, but then it turned into a bad week. Now, it's six months later, and our marriage has changed.

I have gone through the motions of planning the anniversary celebration, numbed at the cold distance that has entered my own. There has been little desire to celebrate someone else's marriage when I wonder if my marriage will even make it to the next year.

I love the man, but our marriage is spiraling, and he won't fight for it.

"Brooks…" I whisper, trying to keep my voice from wavering. He glances through me. He hasn't seen my pain in a long time. Maybe he has been lost in his own, but I've reached the point where I need to start swimming out of this darkness, with or without him.

7

"Brooks…"

His eyes stay glued to his phone.

My chest burns. My lungs only get half breaths as I hold back the sobs I've swallowed for six months, maybe more, because if I'm honest, he stopped noticing me physically once Avery was born. His "good morning, beautiful" came less and less. I chalked it up to being exhausted first-time parents because I also stopped noticing him for a while. I was a new mom, breastfeeding and recovering from giving birth. I didn't have the confidence to notice him. When I finally started feeling like myself again, our marriage felt off. Our once impenetrable relationship felt like it was one disaster away from crumbling.

I thought I could save us, but now I'm not sure. I'm drowning. I have to get up to the surface, for me, but more than anything, for our daughter. I refuse to let this be her definition of love, not when I had the perfect one growing up.

"Brooks Montgomery…" I yell, slamming my hand on the counter. The cold marble stings against my palm, but I welcome the pain. Being able to lose control, if only for a moment, is gratifying.

This time, he looks up. His gaze misses mine by about an inch, but he still doesn't put down that stupid phone. His eyes are cold and hard.

"Is it necessary for you to yell? I'm sitting right here," he asks. Anger and irritation leech into his voice.

I close my eyes and count to ten to control my temper. We can't keep living like this. If I don't say this now, we both might drown, taking our daughter down with us.

"Brooks, I need you to listen to me. Really listen, okay?"

His eyes meet mine this time, softening, "I always listen to you."

"Brooks, just say okay, please." My irritation flames at the lie that easily slipped off his tongue. Once upon a time, it was true, but now conversations happen while his head is buried in paperwork—or worse, a phone.

8

He studies me, wariness creeping into eyes once filled with warmth and love. I cross my arms and straighten my back, unwilling to continue this conversation until I know I have his full attention for once.

"Fine," he says, setting his phone face down and tipping back his chair. He folds his arms across his chest, matching my stance. "Is that better?"

I ignore the sarcasm and study him again—giving myself time to gather the courage to say what I need to. He continues to watch me, our gazes like a clash of swords against one another—and, while I've been yearning for his attention for months, now it feels like too much at once.

"The past six months have been rough," I say. "I know you feel it too. You've always been the guy I can count on to save me from drowning. You're my best friend, but lately, I don't see that man. I cut eight inches of my hair, Brooks. EIGHT INCHES. You didn't even notice. You're short-tempered, and even when you are here, you aren't really here. I can't keep living like this. It's not fair to either of us, especially not to our daughter."

My breath is shaky as I pull it in. I'm not prepared for what I am about to say. Brooks's brow rumples, bringing that steeliness back into his stare, but he remains quiet.

"I don't want this to be the end of our marriage. I want to fight, but I can't do it alone. So – I'm giving you an ultimatum."

"What do you mean an ultimatum? We are fine."

"We aren't fine and haven't been fine for a while. So, we either go see a counselor or—"

"Or what? You'll leave?" His tone is even and controlled. "We don't need a counselor."

My voice breaks. I try to hold back, but if I don't say it now, I never will.

"Maybe I will. I don't know. I just know I'm unhappy with how things are right now."

Silence floats between us. I hold my breath—waiting. I need him to beg me not to go, to tell me he can't live without me.

"Brooks," I say, trying again. "We need counseling. Please, go with me."

Tears burn in my eyes, and I watch him swallow hard, trying to hold back his own, "I would like to think about it."

My breath comes in short spurts, sounding harsh in my ears, and pain rushes through my chest, causing my shoulders to curl around it. It didn't hit me until now that his answer might be no.

"Twenty-two years of knowing one another, five years of marriage, and a three-year-old daughter, and you need time to think about this?"

My cheeks are hot as I consider the gall of this stranger before me. A deep-seated anger burrows its way into the edges of my heart. I'm so tired of feeling like roommates in our marriage.

"Emryn, what do you want me to say? At the moment, I feel like you put a bomb in my lap that I don't know what to do with, so yes, I would like some time to think."

"Fine. You have two days. After that, I will decide for you."

Brooks stares down at his phone screen. A vertical line appears between his brows.

"Twenty-two years, and I get two days? That's hardly enough time to make a decision this big."

"Well, it's all the time you are getting," I say with a shrug, even though my insides are churning.

There's a flicker in his gaze that almost sees me, and then it drops again to his phone lying on the counter. I lift my chin. I need space, and maybe he does too.

"Avery and I will be at my mom's in the meantime."

He jerks his head up, and tears brim his eyes.

"Please don't take her from me," he whispers.

"Brooks, I would never take her from you—not permanently, but I can't keep living like this with you. It's killing me slowly. We will be at my parents' house, but you can see her anytime. She's your daughter too."

He nods, those tears dangerously close to spilling over his eyelashes, and I know if they do, my resolve will crumble.

Stiffening my spine, I step towards the door, hoping he will call me back—fight for me to stay, not just Avery. Another step towards the door; maybe if my footsteps are slow, he'll realize how broken we've both become, but step after step, he lets me walk away.

Tears slip down my face. Every bone in my body calls for me to turn around and memorize the lines of his face one more time, but I refuse to let this man, who doesn't know if I'm worth fighting for, see me cry. I can't heal his pain, but from this moment forward, I will do what I can to heal my own.

———————————

After leaving the kitchen, I packed a bag for Avery and me. Brooks met us at the door, placed a kiss on Avery's head, and left the room without another word to me.

He's angry, but so am I.

Avery had a lot of questions about why we are staying at Grandma and Grandpa's house, and I tried to answer them the best I could. I told her we loved her very much, but her daddy and I needed time apart to make better choices and think about our actions. If the wobble in her chin was any indication, I didn't do a good job of protecting her from this.

Neither of my parents said a word when I showed up with Avery in one hand and our suitcases in another. Instead, Dad took Avery to the park, and Mom is downstairs banging her way through the pots and pans in her kitchen.

11

I'm hiding in my old room like a teenager—wallowing in self-pity. Brooks didn't even try to stop me, and that burns.

Throwing myself down on the bed, I stare around my room and try to pull on any of the comforts it used to bring me.

The decor is classically Southern. The starchiness of the quilt against my skin is the only thing tethering me to reality. It was a gift from my grandmother the year before she passed away. The patchwork pattern matches the pale pink on my walls. While it's beautiful, it's not the well-worn quilt on mine and Brooks's bed. It is unfamiliar, just like our current relationship.

I tilt my head back, staring at the delicate floral wallpaper adorning the wall behind my bed. It's a clear indication of my obsession with all things floral and pink at ten years old. Nothing has changed about this room since then, but everything has changed in me.

The vaulted ceiling rises above my head, and a glass chandelier hangs down from a wooden beam in the center of the room. Two windows overlook a mountain view. My bed has a black wrought iron frame, and a cream rug sets beneath it, taking up a vast portion of the floor. A desk sits against one wall holding memorabilia from high school.

A stuffed animal lies beside me on the bed. My fingers rub through the soft fur as I pick it up and recognize it as one that Brooks won for me at the county fair junior year.

I close my eyes against the image of how he looked in our kitchen, calm and as handsome as ever, his dark hair rumpled adorably from running his hands through it. He doesn't even know he does it.

My heart constricts, and I glare at my phone.

"Call me," I yell, but it stays silent.

Heat pours through my veins, and I throw the stuffed animal I'm holding against the wall, knocking a picture off the corner of my desk.

My legs bounce against the bed in a tantrum—like a toddler that has reached its limits. After working through some of my frustration, I roll off the bed and pick it up.

It's a picture of Brooks and me at a football game senior year. His arm is around me. His hair is rumpled from his helmet, and sweat drips down his temples. He was handsome, even then. I'm smiling at the camera, but Brooks looks at me with a soft gaze and a smile that caresses his lips.

My fingers glide over the picture frame softly. We were two young kids who had no idea that hearts could break.

Heartbreak was the one teenage milestone I was able to skip over. When all my friends were experiencing their first breakup, I had Brooks. Experiencing it as a teenager would have been much easier. Now we have "grown up" worries—debt, our home, our kid.

What happens with all those things if we can't make this work?

I look at the photo of us again. Were we really that happy once?

Now look at me, stuck in my childhood bedroom, and happiness a million years away.

There's a light knock on my door, and Mom sticks her head in.

"Come in," I say, waving her the rest of the way in with one hand and still holding the picture in the other.

She steps into the room, and I take her in. I can only hope that I age as well. Her short blonde hair is styled and falling just shy of her shoulders. The warmth in her blue eyes is a balm to the wounds in my heart.

"Are you ready for food?" She asks. "I made chicken and dumplings."

"I'm not hungry."

She arches her eyebrow and gives me "the look." Even at twenty-eight years old, I have to fight the urge to jump up and follow orders.

"Emryn Grace, I just spent hours cooking you a meal over a hot stove. You need to eat, and I have food. After you eat, you can take a nap. You look tired."

Food and naps cure anything—at least according to my mother.

And—maybe she's right about it for some things, but I am exhausted in every part of my body. It's not the kind of tiredness that sleep can fix. I'm so tired that breathing is a chore.

Despite that, I know she's just worried about me, and I don't want to add to her concern by not eating. I place the picture frame back on the desk and walk over to her, slinging my arm around her waist.

"Okay, Mom. I'll eat."

We walk out of the room together and head to the kitchen without saying a word, but the questions are coming from her. I can feel it. They will be subtle, and she will ask them while she makes me a plate—just like in high school.

I take a seat while she dishes up two plates. The routine of it lightens the tension in me.

I am safe in a way I haven't been in a while. I've had to walk on eggshells in my own home for months, and as I sink into the comfort of Mom's kitchen, I realize I am used to an environment where I feel unsafe to show any chink in my armor. Not that Brooks has ever been abusive to me, but neglect can feel unsafe too.

With that realization, the hesitation in telling Mom everything seems to dissipate. I search to find the exact place I want to start, but the order isn't important when all leads to the same conclusion.

"I think I'm getting a divorce."

She sets my food in front of me and plops into the seat beside me.

I've broken her because I've never seen her plop anywhere in my whole life. She is always elegantly Southern, never misplacing her manners.

"Oh, darling. I'm sure it won't come to that. He isn't going to let you go that easily."

"But he did, Mom. He let me walk out the door today and didn't try to stop me."

My voice breaks, and tears begin to drip down my cheeks. I wipe them away with the back of my hand before placing my hands on the table. Mom's hand falls on top of mine and squeezes it until I look up.

"I don't pretend to have all the answers. Marriage is hard, and it takes work.

"You think I don't know that, Mom? I'm drowning in the hard," I say, leaning back in my chair.

She doesn't react to my outburst but merely squeezes my hand tighter and continues, "I don't know the hurt in your marriage, but Emryn, God does know. That's where you should start."

I push my plate away with more force than I mean to. I have so much anger built up in me right now. It would be therapeutic to take a whole set of dishes and throw them.

"It's been a long time since I've felt like God's been close enough to hear my brokenness."

She pats my hand, gets up, and then pauses in the doorway.

"Who moved then?"

Chapter 2

Brooks

I tip the bottle of beer up against my lips. My mom would be disappointed.

My wife—the girl I have loved my whole life—walked out the door with my baby, and I let her.

The sad reality is that I'm not surprised by myself. I have managed to mess up life for a while now, making wrong decision after wrong decision, and now those decisions are pulling me down, taking away all the things I care about.

My marriage is crumbling, and so is my business. The worst part is I didn't see either of them coming.

I've been working long nights, barely getting any sleep to save my company. So, maybe I've been a little distant at home, but I have employees who rely on me for a job. The weight of that responsibility is like an anchor around my neck, pulling me deeper into the sea. I thought I could fix things—to swim to the light before it was too late—but all I've managed to do is pull my marriage down too.

I didn't tell Emryn what's been happening at work because I didn't want to tell her I failed, but is that any excuse for her walking out? Six months of life being hard, and she can't handle that?

She had to see my stress. Did she choose to ignore it?

Rubbing my hands over the scruff forming on my face, I close my eyes. Blood pounds in my ears as the image of her walking out replays against the back of my eyelids. There was no goodbye, or I love you, but she was beautiful, even as she walked away.

She said I don't notice, but I do. Maybe I don't tell her, but I do notice.

The day she got her hair cut, I was sitting in my office when she came home. She stood in the doorway and tapped her fingers against the frame. I looked up, and a light smile brushed her lips. My breath caught in my chest at that smile. I wanted to tell her she was more beautiful now than she was the day I married her. I wanted to tell her that I love that our daughter has her strawberry blonde hair and my blue eyes—a perfect mixture of both of us. I wanted to tell her everything, but then I got a call from work, and I had to take it. Not that it's any excuse. I need to put more effort into making her feel appreciated, but it shouldn't mean her walking out because I've been busy.

When she left, I went straight to the kitchen. I've stayed planted in this seat, only moving to grab another beer when the previous one runs out.

The motion is monotonous, but what else does one do when their wife drops a bomb in their lap?

I slam the bottle down on the counter, wincing at the sound.

Scrunching my eyes to keep the screen from swimming, I pick up the phone and swipe through my recent calls. Name after name appears, giving credence to what a busy man I've become.

I was busy enough not to notice my marriage failing but not busy enough to have a successful business.

I don't stop scrolling until I reach Emryn's name.

It's at the bottom.

A week ago.

That's the last phone call from my wife. We haven't called one another in a week.

There was a time when we used to talk constantly, just filling in the minute details of our day. Now, we can go an entire week without seeing the other's name light up on our phone screen. That can't mean good things for us. The fact that she walked out can't mean good things for us either, but it seems easier to focus on the phone call.

She gave me an ultimatum, but when she left, she decided for us.

If she wants to leave, that's fine. I can't make her stay, but I have every right to our daughter. I won't be a deadbeat dad like mine.

Pressing my thumb against her name, I wait for it to ring, but it goes to voicemail.

"Good times and bad" don't mean to her what they mean to me.

I set the phone down and replace it with the bottle. The liquid is cool against my throat, and I welcome the buzz it sends to my head.

Right now, I'm glad that Emryn took Avery. I don't want her to see me this way. I witnessed it too many times growing up. I wanted to be better than my dad, but I underestimated the stress of being an adult.

The front doorbell rings, pulling me out of my self-loathing. I'm in no mood for company. If I ignore it, maybe they will go away. I hope they go away. I don't want anyone else to be a witness to my rock-bottom moment.

The doorbell rings again. Whoever it is is persistent, and the pounding that's forming behind my eye can't take the whimsical noise of the doorbell.

I toss the empty bottle in the trash, bracing myself against the counter and then the wall. I see the outline of a man through the glass door and realize it's Emryn's dad, Jonathan. My stomach lurches at the thought of him seeing me like this.

Jonathan stepped into a place my father couldn't fill growing up. If Emryn and I can't make this work, I will lose him too. He will take her side in the separation.

Of course, he will. He's her father. I can understand that. If some punk boy hurt my daughter, there isn't anything I wouldn't do to protect her.

Maybe that's why he's here—to protect her—and if he tried, I would let him knock me out for letting my daughter and wife walk out the door.

Pulling the door open, I only flinch a little when I come face to face with the man.

The punch I'm preparing myself for never comes.

I stay silent because what is there to say?

He stands staring at me, and I know what I must look like because disgust is evident in his eyes, the mirror set to his daughter's.

The five o'clock shadow running across my face is scruffy and starting to itch. I'm still wearing my work clothes from earlier today. The buttons of my shirt are undone at the top, and my tie is askew. I never wear a suit, but today I had a meeting after meeting with the bank. Between the suit, scruff, and edge of a headache forming behind my eyes, I must look like a drunken frat boy.

Jonathan takes a deep breath and shoves his hand into his pocket, shaking his head at me.

He should have punched me.

That would be ten times easier than standing here letting down another important person in my life.

He's the first to break the silence.

"Avery is in the car. By the looks of you, I will let her stay there. She doesn't need to see you like this."

A curt nod is the only response I give. If he is merely here to taunt me with my daughter, then I'm no longer interested in standing here.

I move to shut the door, but he sticks his foot in the jamb before it closes.

"Brooks, you are not this man."

19

I grit my teeth, holding back my temper.

"Maybe you don't know me as well as you think you do."

"I don't know what happened between you and my daughter. Frankly, it isn't my business to know your marriage, but from my perspective, I'm standing here looking at a man who is drunk instead of fighting to make sure that his daughter and wife come back home. I do know you. You will regret it if you lose them for good because you stood back and didn't try."

Silence.

That's all I give him, but inside, his words are like a punch to my stomach.

He shakes his head once more, the disappointment pulling his brows down further against the set of his eyes.

"I've said my piece. I'll leave you with this. You have a little girl who will grow and have you for her definition of love and marriage. You need to think carefully about what you want that definition to be because she is likely to replicate her choice of a spouse through you. I tried hard to instill this in my daughter, and it's something I want you to recognize too. If for no other reason, do it for Avery."

He steps off the porch, leaving me alone, watching as he drives away with my daughter in the car.

My throat aches, making it hard to swallow as she gets further and further away.

Will she ask about me tonight? Will she wonder why I'm not there to read her a bedtime story? Despite how busy I've been, I always kiss her goodnight.

Will my wife notice my absence? Will she sleep on the couch like I plan to do because I don't want to sleep alone in our bed?

These questions plague me.

Returning to the kitchen, I grab my phone, shooting off a quick text to Emryn.

I'll go.

My legs are numb, which is strange, considering the couch I'm sitting on is plush and comfortable. Emryn texted me last week with a therapist's name, address, and appointment time. She didn't waste any time finding one. I've thought about it all week. My emotions range from understanding to anger—but mostly anger.

Nothing is secret in this small town. Southern gossip is the town's biggest type of entertainment, and the gossips have acquired enough to last a lifetime this week. The rough patch in our marriage will jump from person to person and be all over town before we make it out of this appointment. Plus, my business officially declared bankruptcy, and it's only a matter of time before that's the topic of discussion.

I haven't told Emryn yet. Maybe I should have, but when I think about it, I see her walking out our front door and leaving me behind—broken.

My knees bounce up and down, shaking to the thundering rhythm of my heart in my ears.

It's our first appointment and Emryn's late.

I glance around the room, trying to let it distract me. The walls are warm beige, which is surprising. I pictured a therapist's office with the same sterile white walls as any doctor's. The couch I'm sitting on is plush in deep turquoise. The wall in front of me holds my attention above all else. A mural takes up its expanse. In the center of the wall, a man's body is painted from his neck down to his hips. His arms are stretched out wide on either side of his body. On one side, he wears deep purple robes that are worn and tattered. On the other side, he's painted in an immaculate suit. It's not the clothing that holds my attention, though. It's the deeply embedded scars in the palms of his hands. There is raw detail in those scars, jagged and pink, holding the weight of the world's pain.

21

The swoosh of the automatic doors draws my attention from the painting as Emryn rushes in, a flurry of activity. She's juggling her purse, a cup, keys, and papers while her phone is pressed between her shoulder and ear. She doesn't notice me, but that seems to be our problem. The heat of life's troubles dimmed the magnetic field that used to draw us to each other.

As she ends her phone call, her eyes meet mine, and it's one moment I wish she hadn't noticed me.

She knows, and I wish I could sink into the couch and disappear because the hurt in her eyes is one that I've caused. The gossip reached her before I was brave enough to tell her myself. My anger might have ruined any chance of fixing this before we started trying.

I drop my eyes, unable to take the betrayal in hers. Her shoes slip into my line of sight as she steps up next to me.

"Is there something you need to tell me?" she asks.

Still, I don't look up at her.

I shrug one shoulder and say, "Seems like you already know, so what is there to tell you?"

"Look at me when you are talking to me. You at least owe me that," she snaps.

I grind my teeth before lifting my eyes to hers.

"Better?" I ask, condescension floating into my voice.

She doesn't justify my question with a response and asks her own instead, "What are we going to do about our finances?"

"I have it figured out. Don't worry about it."

"Classic, Brooks—always handling everything on his own—never needing anyone else to figure things out. Not even his wife. This involves your daughter and me too. I have a right to know what the plan is."

The door to my right opens before I can answer her, and the therapist ushers us into his room.

Dr. Phelps reminds me of an elderly grandfather. His snow-white hair is so full it can't be contained to his head. Little tufts also stick out from his ears, with bushy eyebrows set above kind eyes. Glasses are precariously perched at the end of his nose, and his gait is slow as he walks into the adjoining room and closes the door behind us.

This room is similar to the last, with warm undertones and plush seating. Despite the room's warmth, the coldness emanating from Emryn sends a deep chill through my bones. Contempt rises like bile in my throat.

Why are we here if she can't look at me with any trace of respect?

I realize I hurt her, but I've been trying to protect her from this. I've been doing everything I can to save the business on my own so she doesn't have to worry—even now, I have a plan for finances until I can find another job. I made good financial decisions for the two years that my business was thriving. I invested and saved. Our house is nearly paid for because I made big payments towards it during that time, and we have no car payments. Our savings account has enough in it that we can make it at least six months without me having a job—probably longer, but I will go insane if I don't have a job before then.

Guilt eats at my stomach as I think about the employees I've left in their own financial situations. I might have prepared my family for this, but did they? I fought hard so they didn't have to worry about it, but I can't fight against a recession.

Emryn and I step further into the room and sit on the couch, taking opposite sides. The physical distance is a blatant reminder of our emotional one.

"Emryn...Brooks, I'm glad that you both are here today. As you know, my name is Dr. Phelps. I have worked in marriage and family counseling for over thirty years. My approach may seem unorthodox to some, but I've seen a lot of success over the years. I avidly promote Christ as the center of every relationship, so if you are uncomfortable with that, I can suggest another counselor."

He pauses long enough to give us a chance to speak up. We both stay silent, and he continues, "If you don't mind, I would like to pray before we start to get to know one another."

Dr. Phelps's voice warbles as he prays for the strength to guide our marriage to a place that serves God.

I rub my knuckles over the scruff of my face, needing something to do before the pressure of everything takes me under.

The prayer ends, and it's a full minute before anyone speaks again. The only sound that fills the room is the roughness of my beard against the callouses on my knuckles.

Claws dig in my chest as I fight against the urge to say something— anything—because I can't handle not being in control.

After my mom died, I was forced to see the school counselor until graduation. I refused to speak in any of those sessions. They called it childhood trauma or some other psycho-analysis babble, but the real reason was much simpler than that—I hated feeling out of control. I didn't want anyone else's help. I could fix myself.

I could have gone my whole life without sitting in another counselor's office, but here we are.

Heat creeps up my neck, and when I think I might explode, Dr. Phelps turns to me and asks, "Brooks, how about we start with you? Why don't you tell me a little about your day today?"

The claws dig deeper, choking me. That is not a question I want to answer today—of all days. This is a setup, and I am trapped.

A derisive snort slips out, and I say, "Well, Doc, let's see. It started this morning when I filed for bankruptcy for my business—a fact that my wife was unaware of until about fifteen minutes ago—and, let's be honest, I'm not sure how I kept it from her until now, seeing as everyone in this town thinks other people's business is their own. Then, after losing something I have been working very hard to keep, I came

24

here to work on something else that is probably beyond saving."

Emryn's inhale is sharp, and my guilt is instant. I don't mean it. At least, I don't want to mean it. I love her, but I'm not sure love is enough to solve all our problems.

There's a small fray at the bottom of the couch, and I make sure my gaze doesn't stray from it. Partially because I don't want to see the hurt in her eyes, but more so because I don't want her to see the anger in mine.

For months, I have been killing myself to save my company and give her everything she's ever wanted at the same time. She wanted a new car. I got it for her. She wanted a bigger house. We moved into one. She wanted to stay home with Avery. I agreed. None of this is to say that Emryn is a bad person—she's not. She's just a little naive, and even that's not *really* her fault. She grew up with a silver spoon. She was spoiled, but not in a mean rich girl kind of way. In fact, her kindness is one of the reasons I fell in love with her, and it remained one of the reasons I wanted to give her everything she ever wanted. It was her naivety about money, though, that kept her asking.

I, on the other hand, grew up poor. My dad was an alcoholic, and my mom was sick. I worked to help pay bills at fourteen years old. I worked hard to get where I am—where I was.

I went to college and earned my engineering degree. I worked construction while I put myself through school and took care of Emryn after we got married. Eventually, using my degree and experience, I started my own construction company. It did well for two years, and then the recession hit. No one is building right now.

I could have asked Emryn's family for help. Jonathan's been running a business for years, but I couldn't ask. I built the business on my own and wanted to save it on my own. That's part of the reason I didn't tell Emryn about it. She would have insisted I ask her dad for help if I had told her.

"Well, that's a great way to start a session," Dr. Phelps says. There's no sarcasm in his tone. He's genuine and not at all annoyed by my rude behavior. "Emryn, would you like to respond to that?"

I still don't look up, but I can feel her gaze. It's like fire burning my skin. I want to wipe off the sting of that one look, but I won't give her the satisfaction.

"I—I just wish you would have told me. Why didn't you trust me enough to tell me?" she whispers.

Dr. Phelps holds up a hand before I can answer her. "Brooks, before you respond, I want you to sit and reflect on your answer. Too often, our answers are not thought provoked but rather reaction provoked."

I do as he asks, but I already know my answer. I didn't need time to think it through. It's all I've been thinking about for weeks.

"I didn't tell you, Emryn, because you expect perfection, and this was far from perfect."

She guffaws, clearly finding humor in my answer, but there's nothing humorous about it. It's our reality. One I'm sick of living.

I lift my eyes to her and remain silent. I want her to recognize how serious I am about this. I can't live in a glass bubble where everything is in the perfect spot, the house is always clean, and we wear plastic smiles anymore—I can't take it.

"I do not have to have things perfect," she claims defensively.

"Then what is it, Emryn? Why do things always have to be just so? Why do things always have to be your way or no way? Where do I fit in in this life? Because we are living your life, and I'm just here as a pawn—ready to be moved at your convenience. I've broken my back to give you everything you've ever asked for, and then *you* choose to walk out. *You* chose to leave home. *You* even chose the therapist we are seeing. So tell me, where do I fit in?"

"That's not fair." She lifts her chin. "I've given up a lot to support your dreams. I have been your cheerleader through all of it, but you

26

only allowed me to see a small part. You kept things from me because you are adamant about doing everything yourself—never willing to let others in. So, yeah, maybe it feels like we are living my life, but I was the only one in our marriage who ever talked about the things I needed. Then I got tired of talking because you never listened anyway, so I stopped. But I'm tired, Brooks. I'm tired of walking on eggshells around one another. Yes, I left, but you pushed me out."

As she spoke, I moved closer to her on the couch—gravitating to her—and now we are face to face. Inches separate our noses, and fury quickens our breaths, making them ragged. My nose is scrunched in disdain, and from the way her eyebrows dip inward, it's not hard to figure out she feels the same way. Despite that, electricity ripples between us. I'm struck by the notion that if things were different, this would be a moment I would want to kiss my wife.

Dr. Phelps's eyes bounce between us before interjecting, "I would like you both to stop for a moment. I believe this has given us a place to start. You both struggle with verbal communication—that much is clear. Maybe it hasn't always been like this, but it is now. You both listen to respond rather than hear. Part of my job is to help you communicate, so I would like to try something. Before the next session, your homework is to write letters to one another. I won't specify what has to be included in these letters. I only ask that you remain honest and open to one another. Do you think you can do that?"

I consider what he's asking for a moment, reluctant to agree. Until then, he seemed content to let us spar back and forth, throwing barbs to see whose jabs the deepest. I'm not sure what kind of therapist that makes him, but it does little to rally my confidence. Words have never been my strong suit. Whether they are verbal or written, this seems to be one more place that I will fail my wife.

Something has to change. What we are doing right now isn't working.

Dr. Phelps is right. This back and forth screaming match is not getting us anywhere. So, it seems the letters are my only hope of communicating with my wife.

Chapter 3

Emryn,

   I'm not naive enough to believe that love should be easy. It's very, very hard. But—aren't things that are hard supposed to be rewarding? When did our love become more complicated than rewarding?

   I think you're right. Our definition of love changes. We grow older and wiser. Life experiences color our views.

   We made all the right steps. We were high school sweethearts. We got married and had a baby, but somehow, we skipped a step. I can't tell you how we moved from love to whatever we have right now. It's not hate. I know that. I could never hate you. Maybe the right word is indifference.

   Can love be indifferent?

   I hope so because that means there's at least love there. But doesn't indifference mean that there is a lack of caring? Because that's not it either. I do care. I want good things for you, Emryn, but I'm exhausted.

   I'm not explaining this well. I do that a lot, and I can see now how that hurts you.

   There was a day, about three months ago, when I came home from work. I was exhausted. It was one of those days when everything went wrong. I wanted nothing more than to come home, sit on the couch, and relax. Then I got home, and you were dressed up. I remember because I noticed. I noticed how beautiful you looked. Your hair was curled, framing your face, and you *were wearing my favorite dress—the olive one that highlights the bronze of your summer tan. I wanted to tell you how my heart raced at the mere sight of you, even after all this time. I tried to place your hand over my chest so you could feel how hard it was beating. I thought it might fall out of my chest at your feet. Before I could pull you to me, you looked at me, and instead of seeing the stress of the bad day I just had, all you saw was my tardiness.*

Your exact words were, "It's like you can't even try, Brooks. You can't even try to care about something important to me."

I am tired of feeling like I can never live up to this perfect picture you've created in your head. I understand that your parents have this all-consuming love. I wanted that for us too, but no matter what I do, I can't seem to live up to that for you.

Instead of telling you how beautiful you were that night, I took my frustration out on you. I made sure you knew I didn't want to go out, even though it had been months since we spent any time alone. I grumbled the entire time I got ready. I grumbled as we were in the car. I grumbled when we arrived at the restaurant. I grumbled for the entirety of that night. I let my bad day ruin your night too. You were a good sport for a while, but then you stopped trying. We ate in silence. We haven't been out since, and if I'm being honest, I didn't notice until you left.

I wonder if our lives would look different if I told you how I felt that night. Would that one day of honesty have led to more from both of us? Would you have tried to understand what I was feeling, or would you have taken offense to the smallest of feelings from me?

Do you know how hard you are to talk to, Em?

I'm constantly competing for your attention. There was a time when I would walk into the room and pull you into a hug, and you wouldn't cringe away from my touch. But now, when I do that same thing, you are quick to pull out of my grasp, pleading that you have supper to cook, laundry to fold, and any other task you can think of so as not to sit and soak up each other's presence for a moment.

So, I stayed quiet. I didn't tell you about my problems.

Yes, I should have told you what was happening. I should have forced the time. But, Em, you should have asked.

You want to place all the blame on me, and I'm willing to shoulder some of it, but I can't take all of it.

I'm willing to fess up and look at my faults. One of them is that I can't stand the thought of you looking at me like my mom used to look at my dad. She lived her whole life for him, and he couldn't even have the decency to give her anything except a drunk for a husband.

I don't want to be that person to you. I want to be better than him. I want you to have everything you ever dreamed of, so I worked harder, even though I was drowning in a riptide of failure.

Your dreams have kept growing, but so have my failures. And the more I failed, the less I felt I could talk to you.

Then you walked out, and it's like someone flipped a light switch on our marriage. One minute, I was convincing myself we were okay, and then the lights were out, and you were gone. Now I'm angry over a situation where I'm unsure who is more to blame.

Brooks

Chapter 4

Emryn

My hands tremble as I fold the letter back into the envelope that it came in. The word indifferent sticks in my mind like a blaring alarm signaling the end. Brooks prefers to be indifferent, but I think that I prefer hate. I would rather he hated me because at least there's emotion there. The numbness is what scares me.

Can a marriage ever recover when someone becomes numb?

I'm not sure.

It's been a week since the therapy session, and outside the texts about Avery's schedule, we don't talk. Nothing has changed. He asks about Avery but never about me.

He misses her.

I've never once disputed him being a good dad. From the beginning, it's been important to him to be better than what he had, and I can't help feeling like I've taken that away from him. I don't want to add to his trauma when it comes to being a dad, but I can see the trauma we will give Avery if we don't try to fix this.

If we can't make our marriage work, we at least have to figure out how to co-parent. So, while we work on our marriage in counseling, we are also working on co-parenting at the park.

Avery and I are sitting on a park bench, waiting for Brooks to arrive.

We decided to spend a few hours together to give her a little normalcy. She's been happy to be with my mom and dad. They spoil her, but she misses home.

The sun warms our skin against the fall wind. I have on jeans and a T-shirt today, but the wind will turn bitter in a few weeks, and the sun will lose some of its power. For now, I'm enjoying the days before summer fades completely into fall.

I look around, pulling a deep breath into my lungs. I haven't gotten a good breath since I left home.

The park is one of the smaller ones in town, with only one set of monkey bars, a swing set, and a slide. It's rarely used anymore, and the equipment needs to be replaced, but it's Avery's favorite. She likes that the slide, which used to be red, has faded to pale pink in the sun.

"Mommy?"

Avery's soft voice draws my attention to her—my light-haired baby, who looks so much like her daddy. From the day I found out I was pregnant, I prayed she would have her daddy's blue eyes. I couldn't imagine anything better than having a replica of Brooks. I never thought there would be a day that those similarities would seem like a bittersweet reminder. I wouldn't change her, but that doesn't mean it doesn't send a few pangs to my heart when I look into eyes that mirror her daddy's.

"Yes, baby?" I ask, smoothing back the ringlet of curls that have escaped her unruly ponytail.

"Has daddy been in time out? Is that why he doesn't tuck me in now?"

Hot tears sting my eyes, and my throat aches. I blink to keep them from spilling over my eyelashes.

I will not cry in front of her, but more than that, I have to stop crying, period. Tears won't make him choose me like he used to.

This is not something a three-year-old should worry about. I decided to leave, not Brooks. He was content to spend our marriage as mere roommates, but one more day of being looked through seemed like torture to me.

Before I can form an answer, she's barreling on.

"My friend Lakelyn says that her daddy took a time out from her mommy when she was born, and now she has a new daddy, but, Mommy, I don't want a new daddy. I love mine already."

Any semblance of control I might have had shatters at her last words. Either choice I make, staying or leaving, I am creating a picture of a broken love for her.

"Avery, your daddy loves you with his *whole* heart. No one will replace that. I know things are a little strange for us right now, but I want you to know that Mommy and Daddy are working on it, okay?"

She nods, content to believe me without further proof. Sometimes, I miss that naivety of implicitly trusting that things will be okay.

In her case, it's true.

We will both do our best to make our daughter feel loved. Things will be okay for her, but I'm not sure they will be okay for me. Brooks is the only man I have ever loved, and I can't imagine that changing.

His truck pulls into the parking lot, and nerves run along my skin, making the fine hairs on my arm stand up.

Avery notices when he gets out of the car. She jumps off the bench and sprints to meet him in the center of the playground. When she reaches him, she flings herself into his arms with no question as to whether he will catch her. I wish I knew he would catch me too.

Rising off the bench, I make my way over to them. I can't help but smile. Brooks as a dad has always been my favorite version of him.

When I get close enough, he gives me a nod of acknowledgment over Avery's head.

I nod back. The air between us is awkward. I can't remember a time since I've known him that I haven't known what to say.

He finally breaks the silence, looking at Avery, "Are you ready to go play?"

She bounces up and down in his arms, bringing a smile to his face.

Taking advantage of his focus on her, I study him for a minute. Dark circles line the underside of his eyes, and his facial hair, usually only a dark scruff, has gotten long and unruly. Even though it's only been a few weeks since I left, his clothes hang from his frame.

He sets Avery down and says, "Okay, lead the way then, turkey."

She takes off, running toward the slides. I follow her, but Brooks grabs my hand in his. Tingles make their way up my arm, causing me to stop in my tracks. I stare at the connection between our hands. It's sad, but I can't remember the last time he held my hand.

"I miss you," he whispers.

My head jerks up at the admission, searching his face for answers neither of us have. There's a hurt in his eyes that reflects my own.

My heart constricts. I've silently begged for those three words. Even before I left, I wanted him to realize that he missed me—that we lived in the same house but might as well have lived in separate states. Now he's said the words I've been craving, but it doesn't feel like it's enough.

Don't get me wrong, I miss him too, but if I go home right now, will anything change, or will we return to being ships passing in the night?

I stay quiet, and he nods before dropping my hand and following Avery to the swings.

The weather around us does not reflect the chill that runs through me as I watch him walk toward our daughter. Why does it feel like I'm constantly on the verge of making the wrong decision?

Squaring my shoulders, I prepare myself to be a happy family for my girl. We are here for Avery today, not to solve our marriage problems. I'm used to pretending that we are happy. I can do it for one more day.

Plastering a fake smile, I make my way over to them. They are already on the swings. He is pushing her, and she looks back at him like he is

Superman. My smile turns a little less fake at the sight.

"Mommy, swing with me. Daddy can push you too."

I sit in the swing beside her and start pumping my legs back and forth.

Turning my head towards her, I say, "I can push myself. See, it's easy. Do you want to try?"

"No, thank you. Daddy could use the exercise. That's why he needs to push you."

Laughter ripples out of me, and the pressure in my chest eases up.

I look at Brooks, who is biting his lip to hold in his grin.

"Well, you heard the lady," I say. "Start pushing."

He hesitates a moment before stepping behind me and placing his hand on my lower back. He pushes me away from him, but not before flames burst across my skin where he touches me.

How can I still react to him this way when our marriage is failing? Does he feel the pinpricks running across his skin?

Each time he pushes me forward, I pump my legs harder until the swing arcs higher and higher. Once I can't stand the tingles running along my spine any longer, I turn to Avery.

"Watch this."

One more push forward, and then I'm jumping—free falling—waiting for my feet to hit solid ground again.

I underestimated how high I was. My feet hit the ground, and my body propels forward. I tuck my head and roll, not fully completing the flip, and instead land flat on my back.

I fight to pull air into my lungs.

When did I get so old? Was jumping from a swing always so hard?

I'm afraid to move. I've not broken anything, but I will be sore tomorrow.

Behind me, Avery begins to laugh, and then Brooks. His laugh is beautiful and deep. It rumbles from the bottom of his chest and spills out of his lips. I usually love his laugh. It's been a long time since I've heard it, but it irritates me that it's coming at my expense. It's silly for me to get mad, but anger bubbles up hot and rapid.

"Why yes, Brooks, I am okay. Thanks for asking."

His laughter stops, and his joy is replaced with confusion.

I stand up, dusting the dirt and grass off my pant legs. I'm being mean. I know I'm being mean, but I'm watching myself from a distance—I can see the train wreck coming, but I am powerless to stop it.

He didn't know I wasn't hurt, and yet he chose to laugh. It would kill him to consider my feelings at all.

Maybe I could have laughed with him had he made sure I wasn't hurt first, but I can't force myself to. It's one more place where he chooses not to notice me.

"I'm sorry."

He says it so low that I almost miss it. My eyes shoot up, looking for his, but he's staring at his boots. All the anger fizzles out of me.

He's sorry for what? Sorry for laughing or sorry for more than that?

That's the problem between us. Even if Avery wasn't here, we don't communicate enough for me to ask him to clarify – not without it turning into a fight.

And the saddest part about that is that he was once my best friend, the person I told everything to.

It's been lonely without his friendship. Now that we are missing that part of our relationship, I don't have that with anyone. There's no one to go to with my heartache.

What about me?

My conscience eats at the guilt inside of me. I used to have someone else I could talk to about life outside of Brooks.

Once upon a time, I wouldn't have thought twice about going to God for comfort in this. In fact, Brooks and I would have been hitting our knees in prayer together, but we both moved, somehow letting it slip lower and lower on our list of priorities. I can't help but wonder if our failure to put God first in our relationship led us here.

————————————

It's pitch black outside as I pull into the driveway of my parent's home. After the park, I ran errands to finish up some last minute details for their anniversary party. My heart ached whenever someone asked me to congratulate Mom and Dad on their upcoming anniversary. It's like salt in the wound every time. Thankfully, the planning is over now, and all that's left is the party itself.

Those thoughts are still fresh in my mind as I jump out of the car and walk around to open the back passenger-side door.

Empty.

The car seat is empty.

Paralyzing fear runs through my body as I stare at where my daughter should be.

The thundering of my heart pounds in my ears as I try to process that Avery isn't there.

Where is she?

Nausea rolls through my stomach as I run through every place I went to today.

Did I leave her at the printers? They have a kid's area there that she likes to play at when we go in.

I was distracted.

What kind of mother am I that I can lose my daughter?

I have to call Brooks. He'll know what to do. He's always calm during my panic.

Then, like lightning striking, I remember that Avery is with him.

Relief washes through my body as I sag to the ground. That relief turns to sobs—big gulping sobs that leave me unable to breathe.

Is this what it's going to be like from now on? Will I have to get used to the days I don't see my daughter? What about holidays and birthdays? Will I have to give those up with her too? Will my husband find someone else—someone he will open up to?

Sliding against the car to the ground, I press my cheek against the coolness of the cement. My adrenaline spiked in the mere seconds I thought I had lost Avery, but now that the moment has passed and the energy drained, it will be a thousand years before I can move from this spot.

Tears slide down my cheek and over the edge of my nose before splattering onto the concrete. My lungs burn from the inability to take a deep breath through my sobs. I should sit up, but I can't, not even when the beam of headlights flashes across me.

I don't look up when I hear a car door slam. I don't move when footsteps thunder against the concrete towards me. I'm frozen in my grief of what the future looks like for my little family.

Strong arms wrap around me, and still, I don't move.

"Oh, baby girl. It's going to be okay. You're going to be okay."

My dad's voice rumbles low and soothing. He sits on the concrete, holding me against him.

Emotions flow out with every teardrop that falls.

Anger. Sadness. Confusion.

Each one builds upon the other, but none can replace the fear. I'm scared. The chance to be fully present in my daughter's life is slipping through my fingers. The man I love may one day love someone else. I'm terrified that I won't be able to control the outcome.

Dad starts to speak, but it isn't to me, "Dear Lord, you know the hurt here. You are the maker of the universe, and you alone are in control."

My shoulders flinch at the word control. I focus on it, letting it bounce around from side to side but never fully grasping it.

I wasn't in control on the days when Brooks came home, his anger simmering right below the surface, or when I begged him to talk to me, to share anything about his day with me. Instead, he answered one of the many calls always coming through to his phone.

Dad's voice is steady and strong, contrasting my quivering.

I want the steadfast confidence he has in how he lays it all before God, never wavering in his belief that things will turn out the way they are meant. There's desperation inside me that yearns for God to take control of the things slipping from my grasp, but how can I ask him to fix the things I've had a hand in breaking?

As a kid, Dad tried to teach me about stewardship. He always reminded me that God lends us the things in our lives, and it's our responsibility to care for them, especially the people. It was hard for me to understand at six, and even to an extent as a teenager. Now—as he sits praying for healing over the things I have broken, I think I finally get it.

My sobs start to subside, and as Daddy sits and holds me, I whisper my own prayer, "I'm sorry I didn't take care of the things you lent to me, Lord."

Chapter 5

B rooks,

I'm angry at you. This isn't a fight and make up kind of anger, either. It's deep-seated and burning.

But, oh, how I miss the times when I thought I was mad at you.

How silly is it that I miss fighting over inconsequential things?

It's not even the fighting I miss, but the part where we laugh over how silly we both have been. I distinctly remember one time we fought. Well, I guess I don't remember the fight because I can't even tell you what it was about, but I do remember after the fight.

We were at a standstill, neither of us speaking. But that night, both of us caved at the same time. You grabbed the ice cream just as I was grabbing the hot fudge. Your eyes widened when you noticed that, without speaking, we were already on the same page, apologizing with dessert. Then, as realization hit you, the biggest grin spread across your face. I loved seeing you like that— so carefree and happy.

I wish ice cream could fix this now.

I always thought we were on the same page. We might not have always expressed exactly what we were thinking, but I prided myself on being able to read you to know what you needed.

Unfortunately, I wasn't as good at that as I thought.

For all my flaws, though, I did see you struggling, and I never expected *perfection. I wanted to be there for you as your wife.*

Do you know what I love most about my parent's marriage, even to this day?

They always picked up where the other was failing.

We haven't done that. I wanted to be there for you, but I needed you to be there for me too.

You say that you noticed me, and maybe you did notice me physically, but you didn't notice where it mattered. I felt like I was constantly 'beating my head against a wall' to keep up.

I made sure the house was clean. I had supper ready for you. I stayed home and took care of Avery. I did all these things, and they were never noticed or appreciated.

You left dirty dishes in the sink for me to put in the dishwasher. You left your clothes on the floor for me to put in the dirty clothes hamper. You walked over clean floors just for me to go behind you and clean them again. I know these actions weren't malicious, but they also weren't attentive.

Think about this for a moment. How would you feel if one day you were working to build a house, and the next day, when you show up, the wind has taken down all the progress you made the day before? So, you repeat the process, build the house stronger than the day before, confident that this time it will last, only to find the next day that it's laying flat again.

That's exactly what it's like for me. Everything I do is on repeat, monotonous, and without merit to everyone around me.

So, as much as I wanted to be there for you, there was a part of me that just couldn't. I resented you a little. I don't care that the house is spotless. I don't care that things are always in the perfect spot. You think I care about those things, but I just want to feel like my life has merit. I want to feel like my actions are valuable because, if I'm honest, it doesn't feel like they are.

I don't want you just to live the life I've dreamed of, Brooks. I want it to be the life that we've built together.

You said I should have asked about what was happening with you, but I did. You just never answered.

I'm hard to talk to. I know that, and sometimes I am stubborn, but in that same breath, you lost respect for me a long time ago. You stopped seeing me as your wife and more as a maid who also happens to be the mother of your daughter. You stopped talking to me. You stopped seeing me, really seeing me.

Brooks, I need that connection. I need to feel like you see me again. I need to feel respected again. Talk to me—please talk to me. I've lost myself in being your wife and a mom to Avery, and I think you've lost who you are too. I need to find myself again, and that's what I plan to do while we have this time apart. I hope when you find yourself again, we've moved in the same direction and not further apart.

Emryn

Chapter 6

Brooks

" Daaadddyyy," Avery's voice rings out through the halls of the house.

My shoulders sag in defeat. I know that tone. She's into something she isn't supposed to and now hopes to avoid getting in trouble for whatever mess she's made. Don't get me wrong, I love that little girl something fierce, but she lives for making messes.

After the park, she wanted to come home with me. I'm glad she did, but now my feet feel like a million tiny stabs are running through them from chasing her through the house, cleaning up mess after mess. At some point, I just gave up and let the clutter stay.

Has the couch always been this comfortable? I know it hasn't been this comfortable the last week I've been sleeping here. Now, it feels like heaven, with soft clouds enveloping the ache in my back. I'm not sure I can convince myself to get up to clean another mess.

I'm pretty sure I have spaghetti in my hair from dinner. I know it's on my shirt—my white shirt. I'm too tired to care. The spaghetti will wash out of my hair tomorrow, and I can bleach the shirt when I finally get to the laundry.

"Daaadddyyy…." Avery's voice rings out louder now.

Slinging my feet onto the floor, I straighten my shoulders and puff out my chest. I am a soldier preparing for the next battle.

I look around the living room. Toys cover every inch. It's a trap waiting for me to pierce the sensitive skin of my foot with a sharp edge anyway I move. Crackers are crushed into fine crumbs on the area rug and there are scribbles on the wall in front of the couch. I'm hoping it's in something washable. I'm not sure when she managed to do that. Any facade of strength leaves me as I look at the mess around me. I groan at the ache in my body standing up. I'm a twenty-eight-year-old man being bested by a three-year-old.

I haven't had time to think about what happened in the park. Actually, I don't know *what* happened at the park. One minute, we were laughing, and then, like a flip of a switch, it was back to being strained and uncomfortable. I don't know how to navigate the version of Emryn that would rather be angry with me than laugh. There was a time when laughing came easy between us.

When we were in sixth grade, I asked her to the formal. It was our first "official" date. We were inseparable from the day I asked her to marry me on the playground, but never anything official. Two weeks before the dance, I asked her to be my date, but this time as my girlfriend. I was awkward, but she didn't seem to mind. She still said yes. I didn't care that all the other guys in my grade were going alone or that half of them still thought girls had cooties. I only cared about making sure I knew how to slow dance. I practiced every night with my mom. The night of the dance, I was ready. But when that first slow song came on, I was so nervous that I stepped on her toes the entire time we danced. It was so bad that one of the teachers offered to get Emryn ice for her feet afterward. We sat on the sideline of the high school gym in hard plastic chairs, watching the others dance while she iced her toes. I wanted to melt into the floor from embarrassment. When I tried apologizing, Emryn threw back her head and laughed, telling me she never pegged me for a dancing man anyway. Then she leaned in and kissed my cheek, her lips feathery light against my skin. Despite having asked her in kindergarten, that was the day I knew I would marry her for real someday.

I've dreamed about that laugh every night this week. It haunts my dreams.

I make my way to Avery's room, soldiering up for whatever mess I'm about to face. To my surprise, it's minimal. Only a few dolls are spread across the floor. I was expecting much worse.

Avery sits in the center of the room at the wooden table and chair Emryn's dad made for her. In the center of the table sits a plastic teapot and cups.

"Daddy, would you like some tea?"

Not waiting for my answer, she picks up the teapot and pretends to pour me a cup.

I sit on the floor beside the table, happy to appease her. I've missed her this week. I called her every night to say goodnight, but it wasn't enough. Having her home feels right. As exhausted as I am, I would take cleaning up messes every night over the silence that fills the house when she is gone.

She hands the cup over and looks up at me, a serious look replacing the usual jovial smile.

"Daddy, we need to talk."

She places her hand on top of mine and raises her eyebrows high. It's clear that she's been studying Emryn when she is getting in trouble because, with how she looks at me through the top of her eyelashes, they could be twins.

I bite the inside of my jaw, trying not to laugh. She is the sassiest three-year-old I have ever met. She gets that from her momma too.

"Oh, yeah? What about?" I ask.

"Well, I know you've been in time out. When I get put in time out, Mommy makes me say sorry. Then I can get up. I think you should say sorry."

The mirth I felt seconds ago fades. I need Emryn here for this. She always has the right words, but it's a place I struggle. Growing up with an alcoholic father taught me to bottle emotions up. That's not what I want for my daughter. I want her to know that her feelings are valid.

"Listen, turkey. Saying sorry is important, but sometimes sorry can't fix the things that are wrong."

She studies me for a moment, trying to understand a topic that is beyond her years. Her bottom lip wobbles, and I only have seconds to guide this conversation to a safe spot.

"Why can't it fix it, Daddy?"

"Because sometimes an apology is just words they don't mean. If someone doesn't change after saying they are sorry, they probably weren't sorry."

"Are you sorry?"

Her question catches me off guard. I'm not prepared for an inquisition from a three year old, but it also causes me to pause. I am sorry. I'm sorry for not trusting Emryn to be that girl from our sixth grade dance who never judged me for messing up.

Avery's chin joins her bottom lip in wobbling, and tears leak out of the corner of her eyes, slipping down her cheeks. My heart shatters into a thousand tiny shards, poking at the inside of my chest.

I scoop her up in my arms, squeezing her close to me.

"Avery, I know things are going on right now that you don't understand, but I want you to know that I love you and your mommy very much. That won't ever change, but I can't promise other things in your life aren't going to change. I promise that if they do, your mommy and I will help you through it, okay?"

She nods her head against my chest, and I squeeze her a little closer, knowing that was the only comfort I could give her right now.

I hold her until the tears stop flowing, and she nods off to sleep. Standing up, I am careful not to wake her. The rough callous on my hands catch on her hair as I push it back from her face. Before I leave,

I place a soft kiss on her forehead and whisper a prayer.

"Please help me fix this."

————————————

"Ow," Avery cries as I pull the brush through her hair. I'm trying to be gentle, but the girl is a rough sleeper.

"Hold still, and it won't pull as bad," I say.

Instead of holding still, she turns her hand and glares at me. "Why don't you just go get Mommy off the porch? She's been standing out there for a long time. She'll be gentle."

I toss the brush down on the couch in defeat. "Fine, go get your mom. She'll stand out there all day if you don't anyway."

Emryn is taking Avery back with her today. She arrived ten minutes ago and has been standing on the porch since then.

I can see her warring with herself—deciding whether to knock or just come in. She's raised her hand to knock four times and then lets it fall back down.

Maybe this makes me a bad guy, but I let her struggle. I didn't make her leave the house—it's as much hers as mine. When she decides she wants to come back, the door is open, but I don't want her to feel like I'm forcing her.

Avery shoots out of the living room to the front foyer and slings the door open before I even get off the couch.

"Hey, Mommy." Avery smiles at her mom, and Emryn crouches down to get on her level. I'm standing off to the side of the living room wall where they can't see me, but I can see them. Selfishly, I want a moment to look at my wife without feeling her disappointment in me.

"Hey, sweet girl. What are you doing opening the door by yourself?" Emryn asks.

"Daddy said I could come get you because you would stand out here all day if I didn't," Avery pauses, leans in dramatically, then whispers in a tone that's not a whisper—more like a whisper-yell, "Plus, Daddy's bad at doing hair. I need you to save me.''

Emryn rolls her lips together, trying to hold back a laugh. Avery doesn't realize how funny she is. Sometimes, it's hard to discipline her because she spouts off with one of her comments, and you have to hold your breath so you don't laugh.

When her laughter is under control, Emryn takes Avery's hand and pulls her close. She makes sure Avery is looking at her before saying, "We've talked about this. No opening the door unless there is an adult with you, even if you know the person on the other side, okay?"

Avery nods, and Emryn stands back up. I take this moment to step out from behind the wall.

"I was watching her the whole time," I say.

Irritation flits across Emryn's face when she looks my way, and I brace myself for a fight.

"Maybe you were, but you weren't in the same room with her. We've been working on that, and I would appreciate it if you would not allow her to run wild while she's with you. I get that you get to be the fun parent most of the time, so—"

"What does that mean?" I ask, interrupting her.

She steps further into the room and closes the door.

"Exactly what I said, Brooks. I'm not saying you aren't a great dad, but you get to have the fun moments. I've had to put her down for naps and make her pick up her toys, brush her teeth, and do everything about parenting that's not so fun while you were at work. I'm not blaming you for that. I've been the one that's been home with her, but you have to step up now. I mean, look at the room around you, Brooks. There are toys everywhere—messes I'm not here to clean up anymore."

I cross my arms over my chest. It's my turn to be irritated.

"Have you tried keeping up with that little tornado?" I ask. "It's impossible."

Emryn scoffs, "I did it every day, Brooks. Every. Single. Day. Maybe

49

now you will understand how much I do for our family."

Taking Avery's hand, she stomps into the living room—leaving me behind.

I'm a tool. She's right, and I hadn't noticed. There wasn't a day that I came home from work where the house looked like it does now. I took for granted how much work she put into keeping our house up, let alone parenting our daughter.

I missed everything she did for us because I was too busy thinking about everything I did for her.

Chapter 7

Emryn

It was late last night when Avery and I got home. I picked her up from Brooks, and then we spent the day running errands. When we got home, I put Avery in bed and then went to my own.

I spent the night lying in bed and listening to the storm rolling in. Thunder roared, shaking the walls, and my thoughts outraced the peaceful sleep I had hoped for.

With each strike of lightning, I tossed and turned, searching for where our marriage went wrong.

The problem is there isn't just one place that I can pinpoint. I know when I let myself recognize that it was failing, but I can't think of just one place that caused our downfall. It was all the little parts of our life. We woke up one day, and the morning was too busy to kiss goodbye. Then the next morning was the same. We were lost to the routine of our day, neither one realizing the cost it would bring to our marriage later.

It isn't that I didn't notice what was happening before that afternoon six months ago, but I thought I had time to fix it. I kept telling myself that I would remember to kiss him tomorrow. It was always tomorrow. Then tomorrow would come, and Avery would need breakfast, or Brooks would get one of his constant phone calls. It was always the little distractions that never seemed significant at the moment, but looking back, I can see how they created a divide between us. Most mornings, we didn't even speak before he left for work.

There was this one morning in particular.

It was one of those mornings where things seemed to pile on one another. Avery had a doctor's appointment, and my alarm didn't go off. Then, none of my clothes fit. Once I finally found something, the pockets kept getting stuck on the door handles. Avery was throwing a fit as I rushed around, trying to get everything together. I managed to make it into the kitchen for a quick breakfast, but Brooks grabbed my arm as I passed him. I was in a hurry, so I tried to shake him off. He held on tighter. Again, I wanted to shake him off, but he kept a hold of my arm. At that point, my frustration hit an all-time high. I swung around to look at him. A wide smile spread across his face, but I was oblivious.

I'd said, "Brooks, I don't have time for games this morning. Let go of my arm."

I watched his face crumple, and he said, "I was just trying to hug you. I'm sorry."

The anger had seeped from my body.

As I lay in bed last night, I continued to remember many mornings like that. Regret filled my stomach—churning it until I thought I might be physically sick.

Maybe I am not the only one that felt like a window in this relationship. Did I ever listen to him, or was I always too busy being a mom to be a wife?

Things with Brooks are not any clearer this morning, but one thing is—there are a lot of times I was snappy, and I think part of it is because I was overwhelmed from being there for everyone else, and I lost sight of who I am in the process.

When I was eighteen, I had a lot of plans. I went away to college for the first two years. Then, the summer before junior year of college,

Brooks proposed. I was consumed with my love for him and didn't want to do long distance anymore. I moved home while we planned a wedding—intending to transfer schools—but I procrastinated because I was ready to start my life with Brooks. College didn't fit into that, so I never went back.

We got married and shortly after had Avery. I stayed at home to be a stay-at-home mom.

Brooks has always been my dream, but I now realize I need dreams outside of him. I need a place where I exist as my own person—not just Brooks's wife and Avery's mom. I've put them first—always. I don't regret that, but it's time to find me.

I placed a lot of my worth in being a good mom to Avery and a wife to Brooks, but when that worth wasn't appreciated, it made my spirit crumble. Some of that is my fault. I placed my value in the hands of a person who is only human himself, and I expected him to be Superman. I put unrealistic expectations on him and was mad when he couldn't live up to them.

Starting today, I'm trying to change the feeling of being lost in someone else because it's the only way Brooks and I will survive.

I'm going to go back to school. I've been thinking about it since the day I walked out of our home. I want Avery to know that it's okay to be in love, but that doesn't mean you have to give up who you are for that love. You can have both.

Returning to school at twenty-eight with a three year old will not be easy, though.

I don't have to worry about finances, so that's one worry off my plate.

Brooks says he has our finances figured out, but I don't want to add any more burdens. Growing up, Mom and Dad set money aside for my brother and my schooling. I used some of the funds for the first two years but haven't touched the money since then. The hard part is finding something where I can be a student and a mom.

The computer blurs in front of me, and I rub my eyes with the back of my hand, feeling a headache forming there. I've been searching for programs since seven this morning, but after three hours, I'm no closer than before.

Throwing my head back against the cushion, I slam my laptop shut and toss it on the couch beside me. I close my eyes against the pain in my head and let my body relax. I haven't slept well since leaving home. Maybe I can take just a minute.

But—as I drift off to sleep, I hear the front door opening.

Cracking open one eye, I see the one distraction I could live without—my brother, Tayte.

Don't get me wrong, I love my older brother, but he can be a real know-it-all sometimes. Growing up, I wanted to be everywhere he was, but with a seven-year age gap, it wasn't practical. I was the annoying kid sister, always hanging around and getting in the way, and he was this stereotypical older brother—always trying to tell me what to do.

I stopped following him around, but he never stopped bossing me around. He is more overbearing than our dad.

When I married Brooks, Tayte told me how big of a mistake he thought I was making. It wasn't that he didn't love Brooks, but he thought we were getting married too young. That came from a thirty-year-old bachelor, so I didn't put much stock in his words. Now, here he is, and I'm sure he's locked and loaded with an I told you so.

He tousles my hair, digging his knuckles into my scalp. I swat at his arm, barely catching it before he pulls away.

"Hey, Tater-tot. What are you up to?"

He winces at his childhood nickname.

"Can't a guy drop by to see his little sister at our old childhood home? Where's the squirt?"

I tilt my chin down and stare at him through the top of my eyelashes.

"Mom and Dad took her out for breakfast," I say. "Do you want to

54

tell me why you are really here?"

He pulls a face—wrinkling his nose and rolling his eyes.

"Maybe we should start with why *you* and Avery are *living* here."

I narrow my eyes at him. "I think you already know why I am here, so why do I need to tell you?"

We stare at one another—neither one willing to break eye contact. I won't break first.

When we were little, he would challenge me to staring contests. The loser had to do the other's chores for a week. I always lost. Eventually, I started practicing in the mirror. I may be a little out of practice now, but I am still confident in my ability to win.

My eyes burn, but I won't give in. I squint, only sheer will and determination keeping my eyes open. The trick is pretending you've blinked.

A staring contest is not the most mature way to get him to recognize that I am an adult, but it's what it's come to. I love him, but I need him to be my friend—not my crazy, over-protective big brother.

I swat my hand in his direction, and he blinks.

"I win," I say, celebrating by throwing my arms above my head and waving them around.

"You cheated."

"...and you're nosy. It's just as bad."

"As your big brother, it's not considered being nosy."

"Oh, yeah? What's it considered then?"

"Being involved."

I try not to roll my eyes, but the force is too strong—they have a mind of their own.

"Fine, you can be involved, but you're getting the minimum story, *and* you won't react as a crazy, overprotective brother. You'll hear me as you would any other friend. Okay?"

I can see the cogs turning in his mind, questioning whether he can live up to this deal, but if he doesn't, he won't get a breath of information from me.

He gives a reluctant nod, and I let out a harsh breath, preparing myself for the pitying looks I know are coming.

"I'm not sure what to say, Tayte. We aren't working anymore. He's always working, and when he's not, he's not really there. Plus, add to the fact that he lied about his business, and—well, as I said, it's just not working."

There's a flash of anger in his eyes, and then, surprisingly, nothing. There's not a hint of judgment there, and until that moment, I didn't realize how much I needed that.

"It's not just his fault. I haven't been present, either. We are in this rut, and I don't know if we will make it out."

"Do you want to make it out?"

There is no hesitation in my answer

"Of course I do. I love him."

He studies me—carefully considering what I've said.

I won't break under his scrutiny.

"Let's start with the business, then," he says, still watching me—waiting for me to break. "How long has it been failing?"

"He didn't say how long it's been going on. If I were to guess, I would say six months. That seems to be when everything took a turn for the worse for us—not that it wasn't already strained before—but that's when things seemed to tick up."

"Why didn't he tell you?"

I consider what Brooks said in therapy.

"He said I have to have everything perfect. He said I wouldn't accept anything less than perfection, and a failing business is far from perfection."

I drop my head into my hands, unable to control the sadness that overtakes me. I hate that my husband feels that he can't show me his flaws.

What kind of wife does that make me?

Not a good one.

The worst part is that when I look back and examine our interactions, I can see how he would feel that way too. It's like a picture film running across the screen of my mind.

There's one where I'm mad because the bed wasn't made right.

Then there is another because I didn't want to go to a business dinner after a long day with Avery.

And another when I wouldn't go outside to play with Avery and Brooks until the whole house was spotless.

The memories keep coming—flitting through my mind—causing me to cringe each time I see myself sinking further into the strive for perfection.

When did I become that person? Why did I stop appreciating the people and the effort they made?

Tears well up in my eyes and slip silently down my cheeks.

"You know what, Tayte?" I ask, my voice breaking. "I don't even blame him. I have been awful. I did expect perfection."

He gets up from the recliner he sat in when he came in and sits beside me. I let my head rest on his shoulder.

"Emryn, I'm not going to defend you. Everyone makes mistakes, but that's just it—everyone makes mistakes, including Brooks. I wasn't inside the walls of your home as things were going wrong, but if I were a betting man, I would say that you both have your faults. The question is, are you both willing to acknowledge and work on those faults."

Puffing out a breath of air, I say, "I can't speak for Brooks, but I know I'm willing. I started with therapy. He's been at the sessions, but I don't know how committed he is to them. Showing up has to speak of his intent—at least a little, but therapy can't fix everything. We have to find who we are outside of our marriage. Brooks has been my identity for so long, and I think the same is true for him. I've been thinking about everything going on with his business, and considering that I don't know if we will stay married at this point, I'm going to get a job.."

"What kind of job?" he asks.

I chew on the inside of my jaw—thinking. It's the same question I've been asking myself. I have no qualifications, but when I was going to school before, I wanted to go into education.

"I think I might sign up to sub. I plan on returning to school—that is if I can ever find a school—so subbing might be a good start."

I'm not prepared for when Tayte jumps up, throwing me off his shoulder and hitting my head. Stars flash in front of my eyes, and it takes me a few seconds to get reoriented.

"Ow, you big oaf. That hurt."

I rub my head and throw a glare his way. Growing up with him as my big brother, I am used to his rushed movements and clumsy gestures, but you would have to be a ninja to avoid it altogether.

"Sorry, I just thought of a way I could help."

I don't respond immediately. From experience, I know that Tayte being helpful isn't always Tayte being helpful. It's better to avoid his help if you can. More times than not, growing up, his ideas ended up with us in trouble. Even as an adult, his ideas aren't that great. Last year at Thanksgiving, he convinced me to hide the turkey that Mom spent all day cooking. It was funny until the dog found the hiding spot. We ended up eating peanut butter sandwiches instead, and now we can't show up early for any holiday dinners.

"Mmmm—I don't know, Tayte."

My protests fall on deaf ears as he waves his hand in front of my face, pushing away my objections.

"No, Emryn. I know what you're going to say. Sometimes, my ideas aren't the greatest, but I can help this time. This is not one of my pranks—I promise."

Seeing his determination, I let out a resigned sigh.

"Fine. I'm listening," I say.

He sits back down beside me, and I scoot far away to avoid getting an elbow to the head again.

"You know how I've had a couple of jobs out of town this past month?" he asks.

I nod my head, not understanding where this is going.

"Well—on my way home last month, I stopped at a buffet to eat."

"Naturally," I say.

He gives my sarcasm a side eye before ignoring me and continuing.

"As I was saying," he continues. "I stopped at a buffet, and there was this man there who was eating alone. Something kept telling me to ask him to join me. He looked, I don't know, lonely, I guess. So I bought his dinner and invited him to sit with me. We got to talking. Do you know what his job is, Emryn?"

"No, Tayte, I don't, but I bet you will tell me."

I'm losing my patience. Tayte can stretch out a story longer than anyone I've ever met.

"He's a Dean at Hanlin University."

"That's the private college over in Greensberg, right?"

"Yeah, it is, which is only forty-five minutes away. I can see if I can get you an interview."

"I don't know. That's probably asking a lot from a guy you just met. You aren't even friends."

"Emryn, it's called networking. He gave me his card and said to reach out if I ever needed anything. Besides, just because you meet with the guy doesn't mean you have to go to that college."

I mull over what he is saying. This path to school isn't going to be easy. It won't hurt to talk to someone.

"Okay, see if you can get a meeting."

Before Tayte left, he said he would message the dean and keep me updated. In the meantime, I applied to be a sub at the school.

Today's my first day.

I'm subbing for a first grade class, and I'm nervous.

Mom agreed to take care of Avery for the day, but even though I know she is with my mom, I cried when I left this morning. Sure—I'm used to letting Avery spend time with my mom and dad, but this feels different—more permanent.

I've spent so long just being a mom that I don't know how not to feel guilty as I try to find myself. The guilt gnaws at my stomach because what if I'm taking away from my daughter—missing moments of her life so I can have my own?

At this point, I'm not sure how I will make it through the day.

There's a knock on my car window, and I start. I'd been sitting in my car, debating whether I should walk into the school or go back home to my daughter.

I turn to the person standing outside my window and see a petite blonde-haired woman looking in at me. She looks several years younger than me, and her short curls bounce as she waves. I give an awkward wave back and roll down my window.

"Hi," the woman chirps when my window is all the way down. "How's it going?"

"Um—fine."

I have to be the most awkward person in the world. Growing up, I wouldn't have had any friends if it wasn't for Brooks. He was my best friend—my only friend. I'm not good at interacting with people—this conversation is proof.

"Are you here to drop a kid off or something?" she asks, looking suspiciously in my back seat. "Because I've got to say, you've been sitting here a long time, and other people might think it's creepy. You know?"

A flush of heat creeps up my neck. "I'm—um—subbing here today. I was just—nervous, I guess."

"Oh, girl. I get that. Just stick with me," she says, opening my door and pulling me out of the car.

I grab my keys and cup, letting her drag me behind her. We speed walk across the parking lot while she greets kids—each one by name.

When we reach the school's front doors, she turns back to me.

"I'm Mia, by the way. I teach kindergarten—my second year teaching, first year here."

"Nice to meet you. I'm Emryn."

"Who are you subbing for today?" she asks.

"Uh—hold on," I say, pulling my phone out of my pocket to check the message from the school. "It's—Mrs. Edwards."

She squeals and claps her hands together. Her energy matches that of a kindergartner. I bet her kids love her.

"You're going to love that class. I had most of the students last year. They are all such dolls. Come on. I'll show you to the classroom."

We stop by the office so I can clock in, and then we are walking down the hallway towards the first job I've ever had.

I fight against the urge to turn around and flee.

Mia stops in front of a door that's decorated with crayons. In the center, it says, "First grade is sharp."

"This is you," she says. Then she turns and points to a door down the hall. "My room is the last one at the end. If you need anything, come find me."

"Thank you for your help," I say.

"Anytime," she calls over her shoulder as she walks down the hall towards her room.

Then, I'm left to face a room full of first-graders.

I peek through the glass window and see the para-professional sitting in the back of the room. The students chatter among themselves, but when I step into the room, conversation stops and their heads whip around. For a moment, I'm frozen in the doorway as several little faces stare back at me.

"Hello," I say.

Blank stares answer me.

"I'm going to be your teacher today. My name is Mrs. Montgomery."

One little girl raises her hand. Her pigtails swing back and forth as she strains to get my attention.

"Yes?" I ask.

"When will Mrs. Edwards be back?"

"I'm not sure."

Another hand shoots up, and then another and another.

Thankfully, I'm prepared for this. Avery always has a thousand questions, and while I try to answer as many as I can, eventually, you have to distract her and get her back on task.

That's the tactic I decide to use here.

I walk over to Mrs. Edwards's desk and see a book I've read to Avery since she was a baby.

"Who wants to read a book?" I ask.

A chorus of cheers resounds through the room, and I sit on the edge of Mrs. Edwards's desk.

As I read to them about a tree that loved a little boy so much that she gave up every piece of herself, two things hit me.

I have loved a boy at the cost of myself, and sitting here in the classroom—with little ears listening intently—I think this could be where I find myself.

Chapter 8

Emryn,
I forgot to appreciate our good memories because I've been stuck in the bad. It's sad how easy that is. We get into a moment of struggle, and it's hard to see past the parts of life we are drowning in. I hate that because we have a lot of good memories. That should have been my focus. I should have never let the bad outweigh our good. So, moving forward, I want to focus on our good instead of wallowing in my mistakes. Here are my top three:

Seeing you become a mom remains my favorite moment we've shared. It isn't just the fact that you gave me Avery, either. Don't get me wrong, I loved that part, but the intimacy between us at that moment is something I will never forget. When they put Avery in your arms for the first time, you looked at me, and pure joy radiated off you. I didn't notice your messy hair or swollen face, which you later pointed out in pictures. I saw the love that swirled in your eyes and how the dimples on your face never disappeared that day because you couldn't stop smiling at everyone there.

My second favorite memory is from college. The first two years you were gone for college, I missed you. We'd never been more than 10 minutes apart, but suddenly, six hours separated us. No one thought we would make it beyond high school, but I appreciated getting to miss you. It gave me a chance to appreciate you even more deeply. I was never as happy during that time as when we could schedule a weekend to meet in the middle. We would spend *all day in whatever random town we chose, and we both prioritized our time. We put our phones away and let it be about us making memories.*

Since you left, I've been thinking about how much I miss you. It's like living long distance again. Only this time, it's worse because you are ten minutes away, and I can't just come to see you. I hadn't realized how you filled all the holes in my life until you were gone. I didn't recognize everything you did to make our house a home. I'm sorry I missed those things. I'm sorry I didn't appreciate you.

Then there's my third. Do you remember when we first got married, and we would sit down at the table every night for dinner? Man, I loved those times. We were intentional about our time then. We made space for one another. We made time for God too. We took turns cooking. You never complained when mine came out burnt. Instead, you would put the biggest smile on your face and tell me how much you loved it. Then, once the food was on the table, we would sit down and pray. That's another thing I'm sorry for. I'm sorry I haven't led faithfully as your husband. There are a lot of places I stopped being intentional in life as stress built up, but the one I regret the most is the way that I let God slip lower and lower on our priority list. I promise I'm working on that too. I want to lead our house faithfully. I want to be the man of God I vowed to be when we married.

I know life isn't always about good memories. I know bad comes with good, but I want to start making good memories with you again. So, this is me asking you to make good memories with me again. Maybe we can start by going on a date—just the two of us.

Brooks

Chapter 9

Emryn

Goosebumps prickle my arms as I step into the freezer section. It's been a few weeks since I've been grocery shopping. I've been subbing most days, but if I don't go today, we'll be eating cardboard. Not that Mom and Dad would mind us eating their food, but I refuse to bum off them any more than I already am. It's already bad enough that I'm living at home again.

"Emryn, is that you?" A voice asks from behind me.

I don't need to turn around to know who it is. Mrs. Evert's voice is unmistakable—loud and colorful, just like her personality. She is Pastor Evert's wife, and boy, is she made to stand out. Her graying hair is often dyed vibrant colors. The color is always dependent on her mood. Today, it's electric blue. I've never seen her wear anything outside of the color pink, and the sheer volume at which she speaks alone warns you she's in a building before you even see her. Despite her eccentricity, she is one of the kindest women I have ever met.

"Hello, Mrs. Evert. How are you?" I ask.

"Oh, darling girl, how nice of you to ask, but the real question is, how are *you?*"

I cringe at the emphasis she places on the word you. I know what she's asking, and it's not about my health. It's not just her, either. It's the whole town.

Marble Falls is a small town. Small enough that everyone in its population knows the most minute detail of your life. I'm surprised I didn't know what was happening with Brooks's business. I think, in a way, I was being deliberately obtuse to protect myself from the struggles in my marriage because there's no way there weren't rumors floating around town before the bankruptcy.

Gossip is a way of life here, and while that sounds malicious, it's never used that way. Last year, Mrs. Taylor, down the street, was diagnosed with breast cancer. She's a widower and never had any kids of her own. By the end of the day, the whole town knew about her cancer, but in that same breath, everyone signed up for a day to either bring food or take her to one of her doctor's appointments.

I know they all mean well, but that still doesn't make it any less uncomfortable when I'm in town, and all eyes seem to be watching—waiting for a breakdown so they can comfort me.

Heck, two days ago, three people alone gave me marriage advice, and frankly, I'm trying to forget some of the disturbing tidbits offered. For my sanity—and innocence—I'm not ready for more advice.

So, instead of answering what I know she is asking, I give her my best Southern smile and divert her attention. "I'm well, but tell me how you are. I haven't seen you in a month of Sundays."

I miss her response as she prattles about what's happening at the weekly Ladies Auxiliary meetings. I'm zoned out, staring at the food in front of me, unable to concentrate. The letter from Brooks this morning has me off balance. I've thought about it since I read it this morning. I was ready for more blame, but I wasn't prepared for Brooks to take some of that blame—or to be asked on a date by my husband.

That step feels wrong. We still have so much to work out.

Wouldn't it be too soon to go on a date when we have barely scratched the surface of our problems?

Dating won't fix things if we can't figure out how we got here in the first place. I don't want the light and fluffy. I need a raw and honest conversation between my husband and me. That won't happen when we are in a public place—especially in our town.

"...well, how about it, dear?"

Mrs. Evert's question pulls me out of my head, but I've missed everything she said. I slip on a polite smile and nod. It's safer than admitting I wasn't listening.

"Oh, I'm so glad you can come over for tea. Give me an hour, and I'll be ready for you," she exclaims, alerting the whole store as she rushes off.

I take back my previous statement. Nodding and smiling are safe in most conversations—except those involving Mrs. Evert. Those require rapt attention.

Resigned, I push the cart around the store, only grabbing the items I know will stay good in the car. While she is the kindest woman I've ever met, she is also a force to be reckoned with. Pleading busyness won't get me out of it now.

I round up the rest of my groceries, checking my list as I make my way to the front.

There's a reason people don't read and walk, though, because as I make it to the bottom of my list, the front of my buggy collides with something solid. A grunt of pain follows the collision, and mortification creeps into my cheeks.

Today. Is. Not. My. Month.

Reluctantly, I let my eyes slide from the shopping list to the person I hit.

When they land on Brooks, I contemplate a hit and run. That's illegal, though, right?

"I knew you were mad at me, but murder with a buggy seems excessive," Brooks quirks.

My lips roll together, trying to hold back my laughter, but when a goofy grin spreads across Brooks's lip, there's no holding it in.

Laughter bubbles out—loud and unbidden.

Tears slip out of the corner of my eyes as I fight to control my breathing, a reaction that is too excessive for the joke.

Brooks's smile turns to a humorous concern as he stares at me as though I have lost my mind.

"I'm sorry," I say between gasping breaths. "It's just—Do you know how long I've felt like slapping you just to get your attention, and here I am, not paying attention and running over you with a buggy."

A dimple pokes in on his cheek, his crooked smile lifting on one side.

But when my eyes fall on him, the laughter dies on my lips.

He's looking at me like he hasn't for a very long time.

There's an admiration there in the way his eyes crinkle at the edges—the lines of his face soft.

My lips lift in an easy smile to match his, and my heart beats quicker.

I've missed him.

I've missed being looked at like this—feeling seen.

"Did you get my letter?" His voice is soft and husky.

I wince. I don't know if I'm ready for what he's asking, but I also don't want him to think I'm unwilling to fight for our marriage. I just don't know if dating is the right step.

I give a sharp nod but remain silent.

"And?" he prods. "What do you think?" There's a hint of excitement in the way he asks. Guilt settles in my belly because I'm not sure I can give him the answer he wants.

The silence stretches between us, taunting us with the fight that is brewing. I'm frozen, stuck between what I want to say and what I think is right for our relationship.

He turns his head away from me and clenches his jaw.

"I guess that's my answer then," he says, pushing his hand through his hair and tugging at the roots. It's his signature move. Instead of talking, he pulls at his hair and buries his emotions down deep.

"Brooks, you didn't even let me say anything."

"You didn't need to say anything. Your silence is answer enough."

Anger bubbles in my stomach, making me sick.

"So when I say nothing, you hear an answer, but when I talk, you don't hear me at all?"

The words come out harsh—an edge clipping each one.

My words aren't the only ones meant to hurt, though. His comes out loud, not quite yelling, but with a tone that is nothing less than menacing.

"You can make me out to be the bad guy, Emryn. Do whatever makes you feel better, but I just wanted to go on a date with my wife."

He turns and walks away, and I'm left staring at his back while the rest of the grocery store stares at me.

———————————————

The store is only a few blocks from Mrs. Evert's home, so I head straight there when I leave.

After my run in with Brooks, I'm not in the mood to be here, but my mom would kill me if I forgot my manners and didn't show up.

When I pull into her driveway, I debate running.

I'm not naive. I know why I'm here. Mrs. Evert wants to discuss my marriage, but I'm tired of talking about it.

Mom and Dad have offered their advice, but what do they know about what I'm going through?

Their marriage is perfect.

As I get out of my car, Mrs. Evert is already on her sun porch, arranging the refreshments. I slow my steps, but she waves me up.

"Hello, Mrs. Evert," I call.

"Susie, dear. Just call me Susie."

The name feels foreign, so I settle on sticking to my manners.

"Yes, ma'am. Thank you for inviting me."

A genuine smile lights up her face as I take the white rocking chair next to hers. A table sits between us with a tray that holds a pitcher of sweet tea, two glasses, and two slices of strawberry shortcake. My teeth ache from the amount of sugar on the plate, but I would never dare turn down a piece of her strawberry shortcake. It has won first place in the county fair for the last ten years.

"So, tell me, Emmie girl, how has life been treating you?"

A bitter scoff escapes before I can stop it. Her brows wrinkle in concern, but she doesn't say anything, letting me take my time to answer.

"Well, I'm sure you've heard about my marriage, so I won't pretend things are happy-go-lucky."

Her rocking chair glides back and forth, mimicking the pace at which she is used to spending her life—slow, without any rush. She doesn't give a response to my bitterness, and I'm content to sit rocking and sipping on my tea.

I've talked about my broken marriage more times than I can count. Mom, Dad, Tayte—they all want to talk—to know when I will return home. The truth is I don't know. I don't have a plan.

I'm lost in my musings when Mrs. Evert clears her throat.

"I would like to tell you a story if you will let me."

I glance at my watch. The grocery store took longer than I thought. Mom has Avery since I had to sub today, so I know she is fine, at least for a little longer. I nod, giving permission for her to continue.

"When Jack and I first moved to Marble Falls, he was a young pastor right out of seminary school after being in the Navy. We came to the town to interview for a position at the church, and we knew immediately that this town was a fit for us. We accepted the position and moved here within a month."

I smile politely, unsure where she's heading with this. She pays me no mind and continues.

"In those first few weeks here, we met a young couple. They had two kids, and to the outside world—everything seemed perfect. When this couple walked in, I was visiting Jack for lunch at the church office. The tension between them was obvious."

Unease settles in the pit of my stomach, but I remain stoic as she continues.

"They wanted Jack to offer them marriage counseling. They were both at the end of their ropes."

"End of their ropes for what? What happened in their marriage to cause them to need counseling?"

She chews on the bottom corner of her lip, considering my question.

"From what I can remember, nothing big happened in their marriage that caused this rift. It was all the little things they forgot about when life got busy. They stopped growing together and started growing separately."

The smile I've kept politely in place slips a little, becoming less genuine. My cheeks hurt.

I can tell where this is going, and while I appreciate it, I don't need tales of true love working out to pacify me. I don't think the story is made up *per se*, but it seems too close to my own. I wonder how many details are being guided so I can see the lesson in my story.

"Did Pastor Evert offer them counseling?"

"Yes, and do you know what he advised at every session?"

I shake my head, remaining silent.

"Every week, he told them to go on one date. Whether a lunch date or a full fancy date on the town, he told them to get out—just the two of them. When you first meet someone, it's new and exciting. You commit to learning everything you can about them, but then, as time goes by, you get into this rut where you think there isn't anything else to learn. But—that just isn't true, Emmie girl."

She pats my knee as she talks, her pink nails a contrast to my black denim pants. She's warm—a grandmother offering comfort and sage advice—but that comfort doesn't reach me.

Sweat slicks my palms, and I wipe them against my jeans as I ask, "Mrs. Evert, have you been reading my mail?"

She lets out a chuckle in surprise.

"No, dear. Why?"

My eyebrow cocks in concentration, studying her before I answer, "I received a letter from Brooks today that asked me to go on a date with him. I turned him down—kind of—we have too much to work out, and I'm just not convinced that dating is the way to do that."

I pause, waiting for her to tell me that this is a conspiracy theory or that she's just nosier than I thought, but neither comes. She just sits, waiting for me to finish my story.

"Here you are, telling me about this *couple* that needed counseling and just so happens to be in a very similar situation as Brooks and me. It seems very coincidental to me. Did Brooks put you up to this?"

This time, her whole face lights up with joy as she smiles at me. Happiness radiates from her eyes.

"Emryn, I assure you neither of those things happened. I did not read your mail, and I have not spoken to Brooks. You may call it coincidental, but do you know what I think?"

"No, ma'am. What do you think?"

"I think God is speaking to you, girl, and you better listen."

I consider what she's saying, but I still have questions.

"One more question," I say. "This couple you mentioned. Did they go on the dates?

"Yes, they sure did."

"And did they work things out?"

Her look turns coy now, and I brace myself for what she will say. If she tells me they didn't work things out, I might cry again, and I'm tired of crying.

"You should ask your mom and dad that. I would assume their answer will be yes."

Chapter 10

Emryn

My conversation with Mrs. Evert made me step back and consider where I'm heading. I need to talk to Brooks, but I also need to speak to my parents.

It's a game of tug-o-war between my gut and my brain. Brooks or Mom and Dad. Which conversation will hold the most weight in deciding the right future?

My fear is holding my relationship with Brooks back, and I don't want that.

I texted him after I left, but I haven't heard back. With our track record, I would guess he's ignoring it.

Our communication is broken. I'm just as much part of the problem as he is, if earlier at the grocery store is any indication, but it's past time we fix this part of our relationship. Maybe it was okay for us to storm off and stay quiet as teenagers. We were still learning what it meant to be in a relationship, but we're too old for that now. We have to learn to communicate, so he is the logical place to start.

But—there's also this whole part of Mom and Dad's life that I didn't know about. They've lived the struggles I'm going through, so maybe they can help.

Plus, I've played a role in the broken communication in my marriage, so if I talk to Brooks without knowing how to fix it, will I make it better or worse?

Frustration bubbles up, heating my neck and face.

When did I become this person incapable of handling my own life?

That realization has me pulling into the driveway of my home fifteen minutes after leaving Mrs. Evert's. A conversation with Mom and Dad will happen, but it's time I start making active decisions in my life.

Emotions turn in my stomach as I walk up to the home we built together.

When we built, we went back and forth many times about our perfect home, but we finally settled on a two-story farmhouse with a wrap-around porch. It's the house I've always dreamed about, with white siding, wood shutters, and a porch that draws you in with its comfort.

I've tried to shut down all my emotions about coming here. I needed to come in with a clear head, but it's hard standing on this porch listening to silence.

There should be the sound of the pitter-patter of our daughter's little feet against the floor as her daddy chases her through the house, laughter spilling between them. Instead, the silence cuts through my veins, causing pain to spill out.

Pulling in a deep breath, I blow out the ache that seems to be permanently lodged in my chest. I can't hold on to the pain if we are going to move forward. It's time to start letting some of it go.

I raise my hand to knock on the door. It's timid and unsure. It's strange knocking on the door of my own house, but I don't feel comfortable barging in. It was the same last time I was here picking Avery up.

A minute passes, but Brooks doesn't come to the door. I knock again, this time a little harder than before, but there's still no answer. His truck is in the driveway. He's home, so why isn't he answering?

I chew on the inside of my cheek, thinking. Then I hear it, the rhythmic *thump...thump...thump* of an ax splitting wood. I follow the sound behind the house toward the timber that lines our backyard.

My heart isn't ready for the sight that greets me. Brooks has his back to me, ax raised high above his head. Light denim jeans stretch over the muscles in his legs. His shirt is tucked into his back pocket, and I can't take my eyes off the way the muscles in his back ripple as he brings the ax down, splitting the wood in two.

He raises the ax above his head again, and this time, my eyes follow the line of his biceps down to his forearms. Corded muscles pop as he moves. The process repeats, and I find my eyes traveling to the back of his neck, where the brim of his baseball cap is turned backward.

I'm in a trance, unable to move. It's been a long time since I've noticed my husband like this, and while I should feel guilty about that, I can't seem to take my eyes off him long enough to feel anything.

The ax slams down, snapping me from my trance. I clear my throat before he can bring it above his head again. He whips around to face me, and I need to tell myself to close my mouth. The man is handsome.

Despite the chill in the air, sweat drips down his face. He uses the back of his hand to wipe it away.

"What are you doing here?" His answer is gruff, and based on our earlier interaction, I don't blame him.

Nerves swirl in my stomach.

"Uh….I was hoping we could talk."

"I think we said all that needed to be said at the store earlier."

"Actually," I huff. "I never said anything, so now I'm here to say what you didn't bother listening to before."

He considers me, tilting his head to the side. I know he's seeing a mom who hasn't slept well in weeks with her hair piled high on her head and baggy clothes over her frame, but the spark of mischief in his eyes makes me hope he sees more.

"Can you put a shirt on for this conversation?"

"I could…but I don't particularly think I will," he smirks.

I puff out a breath of air, refusing to ogle my husband.

"Fine. Can you at least put the ax down?"

This time, a full smile graces his lips, and my knees go a little weak. I've missed that smile—so full of love and warmth. In high school, all it took was a flash of that smile, and I'd skip school for a day of fishing. He could talk me into just about any of his crazy ideas when he looked at me like that.

"What? You think I'm out for payback after you ran over me with the buggy earlier?"

"No, but after this conversation, you might be."

He gives me a deadpan stare, slinging the ax handle over his shoulder like a miner off to work—his bicep flexes with the movement. I squeeze my eyes shut, but a smile slips onto my lips.

I don't know what flipped the switch between the angry man I got this morning and the one standing in front of me right now, but I'm also not going to question it. I *need* this side of him. I've been craving it for a very long time.

"Come on, let's go sit on the back deck." I flip a hand over my shoulder, motioning him to follow me. I don't bother looking back to see if he's following. In this kind of mood, I know he will.

I sit on the porch's bottom step and look at the backyard's mountain view. Brooks stays standing beside the railing, leaning one elbow on the post at the bottom of the stairs. The way he towers over me, ax slung over his shoulder and smirking, is unnerving. I'm out of sorts with him standing beside me shirtless, refusing to put the thing back on.

I pat the stairs beside me. There's a moment of hesitation before he sets the ax down and obliges. I'm not sure if this is better or worse. I can't see him to ogle now, but his overheated arm brushes against my chilled one every time I breathe.

"Why are you here, Emryn?"

Some of the lightness has left his voice, and I wonder if he can feel the sparks running across his arm like I can whenever they touch.

Are those sparks as jarring to him as they are to me?

As husband and wife, sitting beside one another shouldn't be such a shock to my system, but it is. Goosebumps run down the length of my arm, and it's not from the breeze in the air that hints at fall.

"Ask me again, please." It comes out as a whisper, but I know he's heard me when his shoulders tense.

"Ask you what?"

I turn my head to look him in the eyes, leaving the rest of my body where it is. There is barely a whisper of touch between us, but it calms the storm churning inside my stomach.

"Brooks...," I pause to study him. There's a fire burning in his eyes, bringing smoke into the color, "Please ask me again."

With a breath, the tension in his shoulders releases. He moves his hand to my hair, fingers only lightly touching the strands, tucking them behind my ear. My breath catches, sending shivers down my spine. With the other hand, he cradles my face, his touch feather-light.

"Emryn, will you go on a date with me?"

"I would love that."

The corner of his lip ticks up, drawing my attention there. I know I'm staring, but I can't make myself stop. The slight pout of his bottom lip is like a beacon for bad decisions, guiding me to a place I know we aren't ready for. But I don't just *want* to lean in and trace my thumb across the curve there—I *need* to.

I feel my body inching—one inch, two inches, three inches—until his forehead is pressed against mine, and only a breath separates our lips.

He exhales gruffly but remains still.

I can feel the tension in the hand that rests against my cheek. He's waiting for me to give him permission to kiss me. He won't close the distance until he has that.

All I have to do is lean in an inch, and our lips will touch, connecting me to my husband.

Uncertainty swirls in my stomach. We have so many problems. Things that we *need* to discuss. I know if I make this decision, it will only complicate figuring it out, but—oh—I've missed him.

I've missed the intimacy a simple kiss can bring.

The earlier worries remain, but I push them down deep, promising myself to think about them later. I want to be in this moment with my husband, feeling the butterflies in my stomach again. I will give myself this one moment to act like a teenager again with him—to forget the worries—and then, later, I will worry about all our adult responsibilities that we can't avoid.

I lean forward, closing a fraction of the distance between our lips, giving Brooks the permission he's asking for.

There's a change in his eyes when he recognizes that—a fire that I worried had been extinguished.

His hand moves from my face down to the back of my neck, sliding his knuckles across the skin as he does.

My heart beats so erratically that I'm afraid he can hear it.

As he leans forward, ready to break down a barrier between us, my phone rings, shattering the moment like glass.

Brooks jerks away, placing distance between us on the steps.

A deep inhale fills my lungs. We're married. We are allowed to kiss. We were doing nothing wrong, so why does the look on Brooks's face resemble guilt, or maybe it's regret?

The thought cracks a piece of me. Does he regret it because he isn't sure whether we can fix this? I know he asked me on a date, but is he doing it as a last-ditch effort to see if we are salvageable?

White, hot embarrassment crawls up my face. I don't want him to see the tears gathering in the corner of my eyes, so I grab my phone out of my back pocket, giving it all my attention.

Mom's name is blurry.

I slide my thumb over the screen, answering, "Hello."

"Oh, Emryn. I'm glad you answered. Avery was wondering where you were. She's having some separation anxiety, so I promised her I would check in."

"Tell her I'll be there soon, Mom. I'm leaving right now."

"Leaving where, Dear?"

I hesitate, embarrassed to admit where I am after what just happened.

"I'm at the house with Brooks," I mumble.

"Oh—oh my. I'm sorry I interrupted. Don't rush off. I can keep Avery distracted for a little while."

"It's okay. We are finished here."

That statement holds more weight than I want it to.

Hanging up the phone, I turn to Brooks.

"I have to go. Avery is waiting on me."

"Emryn, we need to talk about this."

I nod my head, waving him off.

"We'll talk later, okay?"

We always talk later.

Chapter 11

Brooks

I'm an idiot.

Two times. Two times—I've let my wife walk out without stopping her. I've watched twice as pain marred her pretty face without doing anything about it.

I wanted that kiss. I still want it so deeply there is an ache in my bones.

Why didn't I tell her that? Why didn't I open my mouth and beg her to come home—to figure things out while she wakes up every morning in our home? Why didn't I make sure she knew how much I love her?

The only answer I can come up with is that I'm an idiot. Well, that and I felt guilty. Not for trying to kiss her, but guilty for rushing this, for not working on our problems before I tried to kiss her again. I don't want her to think I don't hear her concerns. It's past time she feels heard, but I've never been good at talking. Growing up, sharing my feelings with another person gave them the power to use it against me. Having an alcoholic for a dad teaches you to keep it in. Emotions are ammo to wound you later.

So, I let her walk out, held it in, and set us ten steps back.

I slam the ax down, letting the wooden handle dig into my palms—relishing in the pain. I should throw on my gloves, but I don't want to. I want to feel something somewhere other than my chest.

81

By the time I'm done, I have a good start to a wood pile and a blister on my hand the size of my palm.

Expending my energy to a physical task is cathartic and worth it, if only because it gives me a mental reprieve for a moment.

I toss the ax down on the pile and sit with my back against a nearby tree.

The sun is moving down the sky as sweat pours into my eyes. I hadn't realized I had been out here so long.

There are other things I need to do—finding a job is at the top of that list—but I needed a moment where that wasn't a concern. I needed a moment where I didn't feel like I was failing my family, unable to provide for them like a man should.

A car door slams in the distance, and my heart rate ticks up.

She's come back.

I jump to my feet, ready to meet her. I won't hesitate to pull her in my arms and kiss her until she knows how I feel about her. I saw that wariness in her eyes when she left.

A lone figure appears at the side of the house, making their way towards me.

Disappointment is replaced with irritation as I realize that it's not her. Instead, it's the one person I try to avoid.

My dad walks toward me in all his glory—scruffy hair that he can't keep combed and a beard peppered with gray. His skin is weathered and wrinkled from years of alcohol abuse.

"Hello, Brooks."

Disgust prickles my skin.

"What do you need? If it's money, I have nothing to give you."

A flash of hurt bolts across his face. I should feel guilty, but I can't. I can't feel many things when it comes to him. There's too much neglect there. When Avery was born, it hit me just how much he failed at being a father. I would do anything to protect my little girl, and despite having times when I worry I'll end up like him, I know nothing in this world can keep me from being there for her.

"I'm not here for money," he grumbles.

"Spit it out then. What is it?"

"I...Well, you see, I—." He scratches the back of his head as if struggling to figure out how to proceed.

He knows that no matter what he says, it won't make me happy. I will find fault in all of it. I know that's petty. I'm a grown man with daddy issues, but that man caused a lot of hurt growing up.

"What? What is it you want, Kip? Because I don't have a whole lot left to give," I yell.

Tension vibrates through my body. When I'm around him, it's like I'm an active volcano ready to erupt at any moment. I try, I really do, but when he's around, I think of my mom. Then I think of every single time he let us both down. In the end, anger comes out instead of grace.

"I wanted to check on you. I've heard the rumors around town. I figured you could use some company," he mumbles to the ground. He's the picture of broken. The world he's created for himself weighs heavily on his shoulders, curving them in. Tears lie on the brim of his eyes, threatening to spill over. I've never seen this man cry before, and that's the part that breaks me.

I slide to the ground, defeated, too tired to hold the burdens I've been carrying. I'll give myself one minute. Then I'll get up and pick them up again.

His hand falls on my shoulder, and I want to shrug it off and push him away, but I let it stay to apologize for my outburst.

A couple of years ago, he decided to get sober. It came on the heels of me refusing to let him be around his granddaughter drunk. I'm proud of him, but this new sobriety doesn't dilute the memory of caring for my dying mother while he stumbled in drunk most nights. So, that leaves us here with moments when he tries to insert himself into my life, and I push back.

"Brooks," he starts. "I know about regret. There are many things I regret. I don't want that for you. I don't want you to be my age and look back at a life you didn't live."

"I'm not you. I didn't drink my life away. I take care of my family."

"From where I'm standing, I don't see any family around for you to take care of."

His words are gruff, hitting the mark I know he intended to. They work their way in, scraping against raw wounds. Heat fills my veins. He doesn't know me, but he knows how to hit every open wound I have. It's his specialty.

"Get out," I point at the side gate, eerily calm. This is the home that I built for my family. I won't take his disrespect here. I had to deal with it as a kid, but I'm a grown adult now. I don't have to.

"Brooks, you may think I'm trying to hurt you, and I don't blame you for that. I haven't given you a lot of reasons to think otherwise, but that is not my intention. Every day of my life, I regret not fighting for your momma. Now she's gone, and it's too late for me to change that. I don't want you to make the same mistakes I did."

When I don't respond, he curtly nods before doing as I ask, leaving me alone again.

It's been three days since the near kiss, followed by the argument with my dad, and I've been planning since that day. I wanted to discount what my dad said, but his voice wormed its way into my head. Now it's stuck. I won't live with the same regret he has.

Emryn and I haven't talked about our date again since she left that day. She agreed to it, though, and there's no way I'm letting her back out of it now, not after almost kissing her. I've thought about it every day since she left here. It permeates my dreams. I wake up with an ache in my chest, knowing it isn't real.

Today's my day to have Avery, and I'm putting my plan into motion. Emryn is dropping her off, and I'm ready for her this time.

I won't fumble the ball.

The first part of my plan is to show Emryn I recognize the places she contributes to our lives. I want her to know I can pick up the slack when she needs me, but that plan is already going haywire. Between applying for jobs and keeping the house clean, it's safe to say neither one is going well.

On the job front, I'm either overqualified because of my experience or underqualified, considering how I led a business to bankruptcy. I don't want to ask Emryn's dad for a job, but it's quickly heading in that direction. For now, we are okay, but the money I managed to save won't last forever.

My pride is the only thing holding me back from asking. My whole life has been about providing for my family, and if I can't do that, then I'm not sure how I will face them. I will not let either of them down more than I already have.

Then there's the house. I never thought I was a messy person by nature until Emryn left. Now I realize how bad I am about leaving things lying around, promising I'll pick them up later. I never meant to be that way, but I can see how frustrating it was for Emryn. It's something I'm working on.

I know there are a lot of other things wrong with our marriage, but I'm implementing my plan in phases—praying that it works.

The doorbell rings before I'm ready.

I'm out of time, so I throw the toy I am holding down on the couch with more force than necessary, then make my way to the door.

Glancing around one last time, I send up a silent prayer that this works. The house isn't perfect, but it's better than it was. I just hope Emryn can see the effort.

The door swings open, and my breath catches. Emryn is beautiful as always, holding Avery on her hip.

The *thud, thud, thud* in my chest stutters. Avery must have fallen asleep in her car seat on the way over. Her hair has static in it and is sticking up everywhere. It clings to Emryn's face, and she laughs as the fine hairs tickle across her cheek. When I close my eyes and dream, this is what I dream of. The fact that it's missing sends anger sizzling like a flame through my veins, not at her, but at my part in why she isn't here.

"Come in."

It comes out like a bark, and I wince at the sound.

Emryn's lips purse, but she doesn't comment on the harshness of my tone. It's yet another thing I need to work on. I'll add it to my list.

She looks around, taking in the space as if it's new to her. Her face scrunches in concentration.

"Did you hire someone to clean?" Her tone is accusatory.

It's on the tip of my tongue to react, to throw back an equally heated comment, but I reign it in. Snippy comments are not part of the plan. Communication is. Plus, it's a fair question. I haven't made much effort in the past.

"I cleaned it. I know it's not perfect, but I realized how much slack I was leaving. I figured it's a good time to make a change."

Her jaw drops, and genuine appreciation fills her eyes.

"Oh, well, it looks nice."

I nod my head, not wanting to make a bigger deal out of it than what it is. The truth is, Emryn kept up with our house every day and never asked for praise. I feel guilty that the one time I do, I'm receiving the recognition she deserves.

I force out a polite thanks, hoping not to bring any more attention to it, and instead, I change the subject.

"What are your plans tonight?" I ask.

She's kneeling on the floor, taking off Avery's shoes, but she pauses and looks up at me in surprise. She fidgets, twirling the shoe strings in between her fingers.

"Um, I don't have any, I guess. Why?"

"I told Avery last time she was here that we would make a fire and roast hot dogs and s'mores tonight. Would you like to join us?"

I try to keep my face from giving away my nerves, schooling it so it remains passive.

She doesn't answer right away. She turns back to Avery, taking off her other shoe and jacket.

"Avery, honey, why don't you put your shoes and jacket in your room for Daddy?"

Little eyes bounce back and forth from my face to Emryn's.

"Okay, Mommy, but will you stay? Please? Daddy makes the best s'mores."

I watch Emryn bend over, kiss our daughter's head, and whisper in her ear. A smile spreads across Avery's face, and Emryn's eyes light up. Tears sting the back of my own, and I realize I would do anything to put that look on Emryn's face again.

How did I ever let myself get so busy I forgot to continue to help her glow like that?

Avery throws her arms around Emryn's neck and then rushes upstairs to her room. When she's gone, Emryn turns back to me, her eyes dimming. My stomach drops. That look doesn't look like she's ready to try. It looks like she's giving up.

"Brooks...I've been thinking a lot since that...umm...well, you know." Heat fills her cheeks. I'm enthralled by the sight. She's so pretty.

"You mean how we almost kissed?" I tease, wiggling my eyebrows up and down.

"Yeah, that," she whispers, glancing up the stairs and watching for Avery.

Her cheeks flame to a deeper red, and despite my fear of where this conversation is going, I can't help but revel in the fact that one near kiss with me has her flustered. Two months ago, she would have cringed at my touch, let alone a kiss, but now there's a spark in her eye. It's subtle, and if I weren't studying her, I would have missed it. It's there nonetheless, and it reminds me of our first kiss.

We were sixteen. I was nervous, sweaty palms and all. When I leaned in and brushed my lips against hers, I had no idea what I was doing, but tingles sparked across my lips, and heat turned Emryn's cheeks a rosy pink. She was glowing with happiness, and I remember thinking I would do anything to keep that look on her face for the rest of my life.

I might have lost sight of that for a while, but seeing that color fill her cheeks again tells me I have to make this plan work. I want her to be *in* love with me again because I realize now that I never stopped loving her. I got lost for a while, but I'm finding my way again. I will make sure she finds her way back to me.

I take a step closer, and she steps back. One more step and her back is against the wall with nowhere to go. I keep a small distance between us, placing my hand on the wall above her head. I'm worried she can hear my heart beating. Her eyes are on the floor.

"Look at me, Emryn," my voice comes out deep and gruff, giving my nerves away. She doesn't lift her gaze—studying my shoes.

This close, I can smell the perfume she wears. Her mom bought it for her sixteenth birthday. She cherished it. It made her feel grown-up. That's the thing about Emryn when she finds something she loves, she does it wholeheartedly, and that's a testament to how much I've screwed up the past year.

With a light touch, I grip her chin and lift it so she looks at me. She opens her mouth to speak, but I cut her off.

"Don't. Don't sit here and pretend you regret almost kissing me because I don't. I don't regret a second of it. I know we have a long way to go, and I'm trying—but I won't ever regret kissing my wife."

I don't let her respond. I close the distance and bring my lips down to hers, and for the first time in months, I can breathe.

Chapter 12

Emryn

I can't breathe. Flames dance across my skin as Brooks drags a fingertip across my cheek, cupping my face.

I have missed this man who knows how to make me feel loved. In his embrace, I'm cherished and safe. It's the other version I fear, the cold and distant one who left me to ponder my worth.

The man in front of me right now is anything but cold. His lips scorch mine in a kiss that feels like home.

A noise from upstairs gives us a one-minute warning before Avery is back down here, questioning what's happening. I'm confused, but she doesn't deserve to be. Brooks pulls his lips from mine, but he doesn't step back. Instead, he leans in again, pressing a kiss against my forehead. The scruff on his face leaves prickles of awareness running along my skin.

"Please stay. I promise we will talk later," he whispers against my skin.

I close my eyes—content to breathe in a moment when worry isn't coursing through my body.

"Okay," I whisper back, "I'll stay."

Little feet hit the top of the stairs, and Brooks takes a step back, placing distance between us. My world is cold again.

When I look up, his eyes flash to mine, and a smirk tugs on the corner of his mouth. I can't help smiling back.

"Mommy, are you gonna stay?" Avery yells as she hops down the steps.

"Yes, baby, I'll stay. Besides, how can I miss out on s'mores?"

"Yes." She makes it to the last step, jumping off and punching her arm in the air.

Brooks sweeps her up in his arms and throws her up. He catches her and then slings her to his back.

I sit back and watch as she yells, "Giddy up, horsey." Then he takes off in a gallop out the back door, appeasing her.

I know he worries about being a good dad to her, but besides my own, I don't think there is a better one out there.

In the backyard, wood is stacked between two trees, and a fire already blazes in the ring. Brooks has chairs around the fire and a table off to the right with food stacked up on it. It's the fairy lights that get me, though. I've been asking him to put those up for months. He kept putting it off, telling me he would get to it when he had time. I gave up and stopped asking. Now, they are woven through the trees, sparkling against the dusk.

I turn to Brooks, and he's already looking at me with a sheepish glint.

"Did you do this?" I ask in awe.

He lifts one shoulder, clearly uncomfortable, "I had the time, but I should have done it the first time you asked me. I should have *made* time for what was important to you."

"Thank you." It comes out as a whisper—my voice is lost in the emotions clogging my throat.

"Mommy, I'm hungry," Avery quips by the fire.

I turn to her, wiping away the tears threatening to spill over my eyelashes. "Okay, baby, let's get you something to eat."

She takes my hand and leads me over to the table where the food is waiting. I grab a bun and a hot dog, skewering it on a roasting stick.

Rough hands cover mine, and I look at Brooks standing beside me.

"You go sit and relax. I'll do this tonight."

He tugs the roasting stick out of my hand and walks to the fire. There's so much happening tonight that I don't know how to process it. I've always been the one to handle the meals—mine, his, and Avery's. I never minded. I enjoyed caring for them, but I can't say there weren't times when I wished to sit down and enjoy my food without worry.

This is an unexpected side of the man standing beside me.

I can't help but wonder if I can trust him. I want to, but a lot is broken about our relationship. He's making an effort now, but I don't know that I trust it to continue when things get comfortable again.

He puts the hot dog over the fire, letting the flames roast it. He flinches as he twirls the stick in his hand, taking care to get all sides of the hot dog. I let my eyes roam from his face down his arm to his hand, searching for his source of pain.

Brooks isn't a man that will ever admit he's hurting. It would give someone too much power over him. I've learned to pay attention.

I zero in on his hand—noticing the scab right away. It takes up his whole palm. It's red around the edges of the scab, and that's concerning.

"Brooks, what did you do to your hand?"

He winces and shuffles his feet.

"I was a little worked up when you left last time. I was—distracted—and started chopping wood without my gloves. The ax handle got the best of me. It's fine."

I roll my eyes and turn on my heel. "Men," I mumble, walking towards the house.

"Hey, where are you going?" Brooks yells behind me, "Don't leave."

"I'll be right back," I call over my shoulder.

Once in the house, I turn towards the stairs and head up.

When I get to our bedroom, I pause. I haven't been in here since I left. The idea of walking into a room where I have slept next to my husband is intimate. But—now he sleeps here alone, and it's like I'm barging in on his space—not ours.

I hesitate one more moment before turning the handle and walking in.

Our wedding photos are the first thing I notice. There's one on each side of the bed. It's the one on my side that holds my attention. I am looking into the camera, a smile lighting up my eyes, but my favorite part is that Brooks is looking at me—just like in the picture from his football game. The corner of his lip is turned up in a soft smile, and a look of pure adoration twinkles in his eyes.

I tear my eyes away, refusing to ruin this night with the worries that creep up, and continue my mission.

Slipping into the en suite, I rummage through the bottom drawer, where I always keep a first aid kit, before heading back outside with peroxide, antibiotic ointment, and gauze in hand.

Brooks watches me as I come back through the door—never letting his gaze leave me as I walk towards him.

He's finished cooking Avery's hot dog, and she sits in her chair, chowing down.

I walk over, take the roasting stick out of his hand, place it to the side, and then take his hand. I drag him over to the other chairs and pull mine close to his.

"Turn your hand over," I say.

"Bossy," he replies, waggling his eyebrows. "It's fine—really."

I narrow my eyes at him and glare. He gets the message and sighs before turning his hand over in mine.

I take my time pouring the peroxide on the wound. It hisses and bubbles. It's clear he let it get infected. The man thinks he's invincible.

After sponging the bubbles away, I gently dab on the antibiotic ointment.

"See," I say, concentrating on wrapping his hand with gauze. "It's okay to let someone take care of you once in a while."

When I'm done, I look up, and the words I'm about to say die on my lips.

Sheer adoration shines on his face. His mouth is quirked up on one side—a silly smile on his lips.

My heart races as contentment warms my veins.

"Daddy, look," Avery yells.

She's made her way over to the toddler trampoline she got last year for Christmas and climbed up on it. Each bounce is the same as the previous, but you would think she is doing Olympic-style tricks from the amount of time she yells at one of us to watch. Most parents might get exasperated with it, but I look at Brooks and smile, reveling in the little girl we created.

"So, how have you been?" Brooks asks, looking at me from the corner of his eye.

The question is innocent, but it's tinged with awkwardness. We no longer know how to have simple conversations, but he's trying.

"I've been—different."

He cocks an eyebrow, studying me, "Oh, yeah? Different how?"

"I—uh, applied for college, actually, and I've been subbing. I don't think I've told you that." I say, shrugging like it's no big deal.

The truth is, I've picked up the phone a hundred times this week to tell him that, but I stopped myself each time. I was afraid. He has so much going on right now. I don't want him to feel like my life is moving on without him. It's how I would feel if the situations were reversed. If I expect him to include me in his decisions, I have to include him in mine. My choice to go back to school affects both of us.

I chance a wary glance his way, and when I look at him, I know my worry was for nothing. He's wearing a smile filled with pride.

"Emryn, that's great. I'm proud of you. You've always wanted to go back."

He takes my hand in his, squeezing it. I squirm under his praise.

"Yeah, thanks. I don't know if I will get in, but I figured it's time I try to find myself again."

His brows knit together.

"What do you mean 'find yourself'? I didn't know you were missing."

I turn my head towards the mountains. "I don't know how to explain it, Brooks. One day I woke up and couldn't remember who I was outside of being a mom and wife. Don't get me wrong. I love being both, but I need to remember who I am. I look at you, and I see you. Not just you as a dad or husband, but I see you as a guy who's an avid hunter and a great carpenter. But who am I?"

He scoffs, and my heart sinks. I know it's hard for him to understand where I'm coming from, but I need him to try.

"We all get lost sometimes, Em. Do you think I'm not lost? I let a whole business fail. I understand the feeling. You could have told me you were feeling that way."

"And what would you have said if I did?"

He's quiet and, for a moment, I'm afraid he isn't going to answer me.

"I would have told you that I see you too. You're kind—and smart—and funny. But I know you are looking for more than that, so I would also tell you that you're the girl that loves to read. In high school—I remember you would sit in the bleachers during my football games and read a book during time outs. Fall is your favorite time of year. You hate coffee but love hot chocolate. You're the girl who never leaves my mind, even when it seems like I'm distracted. But, above all of that, I would tell you that you're the girl who loves Jesus. The one who introduced me to him, even if we have both lost sight of that in recent months."

Tears prickle my eyes as I see myself through my husband's eyes. I blink, trying to keep them from dropping onto my cheeks.

"Thank you for seeing me. I guess I should have asked."

"Yeah, you should have, but I didn't make it easy for you either. Tell me about subbing. You know you don't have to work, right? I'll make sure our finances are taken care of."

"I know, but I enjoy it, actually. Plus, I want to help our family. We are a team, Brooks. I need you to recognize that we are a team."

His Adam's apple bobs as he swallows and works his jaw.

"I've not made communication easy for us, have I?" he asks.

I shake my head. I won't let him take all the blame. "We've both made it difficult."

He nods, pursing his lips as he studies our daughter, now playing in the sandbox, oblivious to all the emotions surrounding us.

"My dad visited the day you were here," he says.

His shoulders lift as if saying that aloud pulled some of the weight off them.

I'm afraid to respond. His dad is always a touchy topic for him, and I've learned to steer clear of it over the years. He brought it up, though, so is it safe to talk about now?

He studies the dirt, and I realize he's trying to talk about something hard for him—a step in the right direction. I *want* him to know I'm here to listen, not to judge.

"What did he want?"

He pushes out a harsh laugh, but I try not to react. He doesn't need my reaction. He needs my empathy.

"That's the thing. He didn't *want* anything."

"What do you mean?"

His shoulders rise then fall, "He came here for me."

I process what he's saying. Throughout our life together, Kip has been a selfish man, never a father to Brooks, even after he sobered up. He's been an excellent grandfather but never a dad.

"How do you feel about that?"

Another shoulder shrug. "I don't know what to feel. Why now? Why

96

come around now when I have nothing left to offer?"

"I don't know, Brooks. Maybe that's the good part. You have nothing to offer him, yet he came anyway. He didn't do it because of what you have but because of what you didn't. I think that says a lot."

He hums a response. I can tell he needs time to process this conversation and to take in what I've said, so I change the topic and hope he will talk to me again when he's ready.

"Speaking of parents, I learned something new about mine."

"Oh, yeah?" he laughs. "Did you learn they are secretly spies on a mission to save the world?"

I laugh with him because that idea seems more reasonable than what Mrs. Evert told me.

"Actually, they almost got divorced."

His laugh comes to a screeching halt.

"What? Who told you that?"

"Mrs. Evert. It was when Tayte and I were young."

"Have you talked to them about it?"

It's my turn to shrug.

"I haven't had a chance. I didn't want to talk to them about it when Avery was around, and with subbing, I've been too exhausted by the time I've gotten her in bed each night. I was going to talk to them tonight after I dropped her off here."

He nods absently, "I'm having a hard time reconciling that with what I know about your parents. All I can remember is love between them."

"I don't think the absence of love was the problem," I say, "I think they had to make choices that made sure they were still actively *showing* that love."

"Do you think we can do that?" he asks, emotions thickening his voice.

"I hope so," I whisper back.

Chapter 13

Brooks,

What was that? What was last night? You kissed me, Brooks. YOU. KISSED. ME.

I can't stop thinking about how your lips felt against mine, reminding me of the soft side underneath your hard exterior. Then I think about how long it's been since we've kissed and the reasons for that, and I don't know how to feel.

On the one hand, last night was easy. Laughing and talking with you helped heal a piece of me. It's the first time in months I haven't worried about anything. I let myself be in the moment with you, and it felt so good. I want more moments like that. Gosh, that's cheesy, but it's true.

On the other hand, we have so much to work on.

The last few weeks, I didn't think we would ever be in a place to laugh with each other again. I was afraid we were stuck in a place where communication was minimal. So, last night, laughing and talking was nice. I was content for the first time in a long time. At the same time, I'm worried that we are skipping past the bad parts. If we ignore that and forget to fix those pieces of us, will we end up here again?

I can't take being here again, so let's slow down, okay? Let's slow down so that when we are finally in a spot for things to be good again, we don't have to worry about the bumps in the road being ones that will destroy us. I don't want us to stop moving forward, but let's take our time and get to know *one another again, specifically the things we need from each other. Here are three things I need from you in our relationship:*

1. *I need recognition. I don't need a thank you for every single thing I do, but I do need you to recognize that my time is important.*
2. *I need you to be present when you are home. You're attentive now, but I don't want that to change when you get another job. It will be there tomorrow, but we aren't guaranteed tomorrow. I felt like I had to compete for your attention, and I don't want to have to compete. I understand that things come up sometimes, but I need you to have a better balance.*
3. *This one is the most important, so pay attention. I NEED you to stop taking things on by yourself. I know you had to do that growing up, but you don't have to now, okay? I'm here for you. I want you to lean on me when you need to. I understand old habits die hard, but you don't have to hide things from me.*

This relationship can't just be about the things I need. You have to tell me what it is you need too. I've thought about it, and I think you see it as a weakness to need things from other people, but it's not, Brooks. It doesn't make you weak that you need to rely on your wife or anyone else for that matter. You've always been a safe space for me, someone I can depend on to help me dream. Let me be that for you. You have family that loves you so much. We don't see you as a failure. I need you to know that. You can't control the world, and that's the thing—sometimes, the world will knock you down no matter how hard you fight against it. When you have people fighting in your corner, it's easier to stand up after you've been knocked around. Don't hide from the people who want to be in your corner.

Emryn

Chapter 14

Emryn

I finish folding the letter, slipping it into the envelope on my desk. I'll drop it off at the house later today when I know Brooks isn't home. It feels too intimate to hand-deliver it—let alone to stick around and watch him read it.

Avery is down for a nap, and Mom and Dad are both home.

It's past time we talked.

Sneaking down the stairs, I avoid the last one that squeaks. Avery is grumpy when she misses her nap, and I won't be the one to wake her up—even if it means nearly breaking my neck to skip a stair.

Once I'm safely down, I stop outside the kitchen doorway—shaking the nerves from my hands.

The conversation we are about to have is complicated.

I thought I knew everything about my mom. We've never had secrets, but discovering they had marriage troubles makes me wonder what else I don't know.

Gathering my courage, I step further into the room.

My mom and dad sit at the table, sipping a glass of sweet tea. Dad is engrossed in the newspaper while Mom reads a book.

As I approach the table, Mom glances up, a smile lighting up her face.

"Emryn, come sit. Avery told us about your night. It seems you guys had a good time." Hope leaks into her voice as she studies me.

I try not to squirm under her scrutiny. Instead, I lift one shoulder, hoping it comes off as nonchalant. I don't want anyone getting too many ideas—especially Avery.

She's too little to understand what's happening. Aside from the fact that we are being good co-parents right now, I've tried to keep her out of it as much as possible. Brooks and I still have a lot to work out, and I'm not comfortable going back home yet. I want Avery to see Brooks and I get along, but I can't feed into her hope that things are returning to normal. Her little heart will break if I give her hope and we don't work things out. She's too young to process such big emotions.

If I'm honest, I'm protecting myself too. I don't want Mom feeding my hope, either. Brooks has done that enough already. That kiss messed with my clarity. The man knows how to kiss—good enough to make you forget your name—but I can't let that influence my decisions. There's too much at stake.

"Well, tell us about it," she prods.

I cross my arms, irritated that she can't take the hint and leave well enough alone. Sometimes, she still sees me as a little girl, and I can't help but wonder if that's why she never told me about her marital problems.

"It was nice," I reply.

My tone makes it clear I'm not willing to discuss this anymore, but Mom ignores it and continues to push.

"What was nice about it? I swear, I always feel like I'm in the dark in your life anymore. You never tell me anything."

"Ha—that's funny coming from you."

Dad folds his newspaper and looks at me over the top of his reading glasses that sit low on his nose. He squints his eyes, and I know I'm pushing boundaries.

I may not be a teenager, but one look has me backing off.

This conversation is not going how I planned it. I wanted to come into this calm, but my nerves are frazzled.

How does one ask their parents if they lied to them their whole life?

Maybe lie is a strong word. They didn't lie outright, but they didn't tell me either—even when it was clear that Brooks and I were heading down the same path.

"You obviously have something on your mind," he rumbles.

I pick at the wood on the corner of the table, refusing to make eye contact.

"Why don't you get it off your chest before this goes further and things are said that you don't mean?"

"Mrs. Evert told me."

"Told you what?" Mom asks carefully.

"You know what, Mom," I say.

Her hand, which had been fiddling with her necklace, freezes. Beside her, my dad clears his throat. Shock registers on both their faces.

I'm over the shock. Now I'm frustrated—at myself for not giving them a chance to tell me sooner and at them for not telling me before my marriage was in trouble. Brooks and I made our own decisions, but I can't help wondering if my parents were honest about their struggles when I was growing up, would I view marriage differently?

Mom breaks the silence around us.

"We tried to tell you, but you haven't been in a place to listen to us the last few months."

Dipping my head, heat flares across my cheeks. A little of the anger deflates from my chest because she's right. They've tried to offer advice several times, but I didn't want to hear it.

I didn't think they would know what I was going through. But— there were other times they could have told me, preferably before I felt isolated from all the important people in my life.

"I didn't want to talk about it. I was embarrassed," I argue. I look at my dad. "You've taught me to be a steward in my relationship with

God and my marriage. I felt like I failed at both. Now I find out you've gone through something similar, and I can't help but be hurt because you didn't tell me sooner."

Dad grabs my hand, "We wanted to protect you, but I can see now that's not what we did. We gave you an unrealistic view of love and marriage. We didn't let you see us struggle. Now you have this unrealistic expectation of love and marriage—yourself too. For that, I am sorry."

I rub my thumb over the aged wooden table. It's been in my family for years—survived many families sitting there. I'd hoped to have it in my home someday.

There's a war inside me that doesn't know how to feel about what Dad's said. On the one hand, growing up, I never questioned if I was loved, and when I compare my upbringing to Brooks's, I would choose it every time. At the same time, the betrayal of them keeping something from me stings deep in my chest.

"I'm a mom, Dad. I know what it's like to want to protect your kid. I would do anything to protect Avery. I'm not mad that you made the decision you thought was best at the time, but I can't say it hasn't affected me either."

He hums, rubbing fingers over the scruff of his jaw as he thinks. It's a move I've seen him make a lot over the years. He was never one to lose his temper or say things out of turn. He's always stopped to think before he gives a response. As a teenager, it was infuriating, but now I can appreciate that he is intentional with his words.

"We understand that," he replies, looking at my mom, who nods in agreement. "If I were in your shoes, I would be upset. I think by not telling you, we made you a little naive. I'm not saying that's bad, but you also didn't have to face many hard things growing up."

"You think because I didn't struggle growing up, I don't know how to handle it now?" The thought stings, and then another hits me. "Do you think I just gave up and walked away from my marriage? Because I didn't."

"That's not what we think at all," Mom jumps in.

"Then what do you think?" My voice is louder than I intended, but I'm finding it hard to hold onto control. I'm calm, then I'm angry. I'm not sure which emotion will win out when this is over.

I left because Brooks refused to see our problems while I lived there. I left because I want my daughter to know what a healthy marriage looks like. Sitting here, talking to them, it feels like they are accusing me of leaving because I didn't know how to fight for my marriage, and part of me is angry because maybe they are right.

My mom is patient as she responds to my irritation, "We think that you were faced with making a hard decision no matter which way you chose. We've stood where you are, darling girl, and we know the impossibility of that choice."

I take a deep breath, exhaling it slowly and letting my shoulders fall, "Maybe you should tell me your story so I can understand—because right now, I don't."

They look at each other, a silent conversation flowing between them. It makes me feel like a kid again, waiting for a punishment to be doled out.

"Okay, but hearing both sides of the story will be helpful. How about I tell you things from my side, and then your dad can tell you his?"

I nod, urging her to continue.

Mom clears her throat and says, "We got married right out of high school because we loved each other, and we thought love was all it took to make a marriage work. We were naive in a lot of ways. When it was just us—our relationship was great. Now, that's not to say we never fought, just that we took the time to work those fights out, or maybe we *had* the time to work them out."

She pauses, letting that soak in, and then continues, "Things were different when Tayte came along, harder, but still, we made them work. We *thought* we were making them work. It wasn't until you came along that we suddenly stopped and realized we were living separate lives. There was no big argument that led us to that point. We both woke up one day and realized things weren't working. This is where our viewpoints probably differ a little. I felt like I had three kids to care for instead of two. I didn't see him as my husband anymore. I saw him as a mess I had to clean up. I resented him for making my life harder, even though I never asked him to make it easier."

"Why didn't you ask him?" I ask.

The question should be simple. It's a question I've asked myself a hundred times. Why didn't I ask Brooks for help? Why wasn't I more vocal about what I needed from him? The answer, for me at least, is hard to face. I've thought about it a lot since I left.

I trusted Brooks, but not enough to explain what I was feeling. I still needed him to see me as that young girl who didn't have stretch marks or mommy meltdowns. That girl was someone who rarely struggled in life because everything came easy. I needed him to see me that way because I could no longer see myself like that. It would be like saying goodbye to her forever if I told him I was struggling. So, instead, I let myself get further lost in the chaos.

Mom chews on her bottom lip and says, "My reasons are probably different than yours. My momma taught me to be a homemaker, and before I go on, there is nothing wrong with that. I loved my time at home but felt like I failed if I asked for breaks. So, I kept quiet, and that was my real failure. I didn't tell my husband what I needed. Instead, I expected him to read my mind."

Dad reaches over and squeezes her hand. She lifts her eyes to his, and the love is palpable. It makes me want to bottle that feeling up—to protect it from the harsh world outside.

The thought hits me with a sharp pang. Even though I can't bottle love up, there are still ways to protect it. Love has to be cultivated to grow. My parents are proof of that. It's not a seed you can plant in the ground and hope it survives. It requires constant attention and care.

Dad's voice is like gravel when he responds, "I made peace with this part of our life long ago—we both have—but it never makes it easier looking back on it and realizing that we lived it. I've loved your mom for a long time. I loved her even more when she gave me you and your brother, but love is not easy. Despite loving her, there were times when my actions reflected how I wanted to love her—not how she needed to be loved. That, my dear, makes all the difference."

I lean back in my chair. There's only one answer I really want.

"So, how did you fix it?" I ask my dad.

"I wish I had just one thing that could fix this for you, but it's not that simple," he pauses, rubbing his thumb under his chin as he thinks, before continuing, "Even now, it's a constant reflection on our actions. I catch myself stopping and thinking whether I am making the effort that makes me happy or the kind that makes your mom happy. I will tell you that you must be willing to continue getting to know your husband—and the same for him. People change as they get older. I knew the eighteen year old girl your mom was, but I also want to know who she is when she's eighty. That requires me to sit and talk with her—even if it's just about our day. I still try to take her out on dates, just the two of us, so we can get to know each other without distractions."

"Do you think going on dates made the difference for you two?" I ask.

"I can't say it was the only thing that made a difference. We make intentional daily choices to be better spouses, but I can tell you that it helped me fall in love with your mother again. I never stopped loving her, but I needed to be *in* love with her again."

I stare out the window as I think about what he's said, "Brooks wants to go on a date, but I'm not sure if it's a good idea."

"Why, sweetheart?" Mom asks.

"Because what if it doesn't work? What if he only likes the girl I was at nineteen and not the woman I am at twenty-eight? What if he loves me but never falls back *in* love with me?" I whisper.

With a swiftness I'm unprepared for, my parents stand and wrap me in their arms. The comfort of their embrace somehow holds all my broken pieces together. The last of the anger I've been holding onto during this conversation drifts away as their love pours into me.

"Oh, honey," Mom whispers against my hair, "I don't think that will happen. That boy has loved you through many stages in life. There's no way he won't appreciate the woman you are now, but you won't know for sure unless you try."

"I'm scared, Mom," I whisper.

"I know, sweetie. I know. Love is scary. When you love someone, you're giving your whole heart to them and trusting them not to break it, but, Emryn, when it's the right love, the struggle is worth it. Go on that date and see for yourself."

I know she's right. I owe it to myself and Brooks to go on this date and see if our story can work out like my parents.

———————

The bell rings, signaling the end of the day, and I could not be more thankful.

I started the day off on a high note—subbing for Kindergarten in the room across from Mia's.

When I entered the room, their sweet little faces were like cherubs. Mia tried to warn me this morning that today might be crazy since it's the last day before fall break, but I waved her off, thinking she was exaggerating.

I should have listened.

Within ten minutes of being in the classroom, I heard meowing coming from the backpack area. When I investigated, I found a small kitten in a unicorn backpack. It took me five minutes to figure out whose bag it was. There was not an ounce of remorse on the little girl's face. She didn't understand what she did wrong since her bag was unzipped and the kitten had air.

I wasn't sure how to argue with that—so I let the principal handle that one. For the life of me, I cannot figure out how she managed to sneak it past her mom and the bus driver before getting caught.

The antics didn't end there, though. Between boys jumping off desks and using the playground as their bathroom, I've decided I don't know how boy moms survive.

Now I need a nap.

Stepping into the hall, I notice Mia leaving her classroom. I lift my hand in greeting and turn back to the door to check that it's locked.

"Tough day?" Mia asks from beside me.

I throw her a glance. "You have no idea."

She tilts her head back, blonde curls billowing around her, and laughs. It's whimsical.

"Actually," she says. "I do have somewhat of an idea. Kindergarten is a fun age, but they can be a handful sometimes. Plus—they are blunt to a fault."

"You can say that again," I say. "One told me I should nap because the bags under my eyes mean I'm tired."

An unladylike snort slips from Mia's nose, and I can't help but laugh with her.

"Well—a nap can fix a lot of things for me," she says. "But do you know what else fixes everything?"

I shake my head—not knowing where she's going with this.

"Mexican." She waggles her eyebrows and asks, "Do you want to grab some? My treat."

I hesitate. Mia seems like a nice girl—she's helped me a lot since I've started subbing, but Avery is at home with my mom again. I've been spending a lot of time away from her.

Mia must take my hesitation as an answer because she waves me off and says, "You know what, you're busy. It's fine."

She turns to go, and I reach out to stop her. "Mia, it's not that—it's just my daughter is at home with my mom, and she has a lot of changes going on. I'm having a hard time being away from her for so long."

Chewing on the inside of her cheek, she studies me, and I can't help but wonder if there is more to Mia than the fun-loving Kindergarten teacher that she portrays. Underneath the smile she beams at everyone, there's a loneliness in her eyes that I didn't notice before.

Maybe I'm not the only one who struggles to make friends. Perhaps finding a friend is my next step in discovering who I am outside of Brooks.

"You know what, Mexican sounds great, but is it okay if Avery comes with us?"

The shadow that dimmed her eyes slides away, and the sparkle is back—a genuine smile on her face. "That would be great."

Chapter 15

Brooks

My truck idles as I stare at the building in front of me. It's an old country church wrapped in wood siding with flecks of white paint chipping off everywhere. The steeple looms high in the sky—taunting me.

It's picturesque in a haunted kind of way, or maybe it's just that I'm haunted by the memory of this place—the one I keep tucked away in a neat little box.

The thing about boxes is that no matter how tight you lock them, there's always a key to open them somewhere.

As I sit and stare at the church, the key starts to turn, and the memory I despise the most flits through my mind—pulling at the edges until all I can see is the innocent boy I was the first time I came here. That innocence died that day as I stood outside this church, waiting for my dad to save me.

I fight the urge to put my truck in drive and go home. I don't belong here.

Coming here with Emryn over the years, I was able to pretend that this place was nothing more than a building, but on my own, the facade crumbled.

Alone, I'm small and weak—far from the man I've become.

The first time I was here, my mom was lying in a coffin on the front altar, and even though I would love to keep that memory neatly tucked away, I realize that I've locked up too many boxes over the years—letting them build and build until I'm on the brink of explosion.

I was fifteen when she died, but I've never felt more like a child than I did the day of her funeral.

My dad was nowhere to be found, probably drinking away his misery, and I was left to deal with my mom's death alone.

While I sat alone, begging God for the nightmare to end, I decided it was too risky to rely on anyone else. I had trusted my dad enough to believe he would show up on the day my world was breaking, and he chose to get drunk instead.

I learned my lesson.

People can't hurt you if you do things on your own.

I've lived by that rule since then. However, I'm realizing that while the mental wall I placed around myself might have protected me, it also kept Emryn out.

The thing is, I should have recognized it sooner because someone did show up for me, but I was too angry and hurt to see it.

As I stood outside the church, as a fifteen-year-old kid, Jonathan walked out and stood beside me.

I thought he had come to force me to walk inside and face my reality, but instead, he stood there with me, silently waiting until I was ready.

When I finally talked myself into walking through the doors, he placed his hand on my shoulder and stayed by my side.

My dad never did show up that day, but Jonathan Bennet did.

It's one of the many things he's done for me, and because of that, he has always been an example of the man I want to be.

It's the thing that gives me the courage to turn my truck off now and step out the door.

The church bells chime as my foot hits the gravel, so I pick up my pace, not wanting to be late now that I'm out of the truck.

I push my fingers through my hair, pulling at the roots as I walk. I'm a grown man, but standing on the stoop of this church, I still feel like that lost little boy I was thirteen years ago.

Taking a deep breath, I reach for the door handle and step inside.

The interior matches the outside—beautiful, haunted.

There's a path worn in the carpet from the pews to the altar, a testament to how often the congregation has hit its knees in prayer, and a cross hangs on the wall behind the altar, a deep purple robe draped around it. The pews are filled, and as the door closes behind me, eyes from the congregation turn to meet mine.

There's a moment of hesitation when I think about turning around and going right back out the door I just came in, but then pink hair pops up out of the crowd. Mrs. Evert slides out of her pew and meets me in the aisle.

Her hand cups my jaw, and she says, "It's nice to see you here. We've missed you."

I swallow around the knot in my throat, and she pulls me down the aisle to her pew. Eyes follow us, filled with curiosity and pity—both for the boy who was here at fifteen and the man I am now.

We sit down, and Mrs. Evert leans over and whispers, "Don't mind them. They just care about you."

I nod, but I'm not convinced. I think they are just nosy.

The choir begins to sing, and I let my eyes wander to the faces around me. Emryn's mom and dad are in the pew directly across ours, but Avery and Emryn aren't with them.

I didn't expect them to be, but I'd hoped to see them today.

The singing ends, and Pastor Evert steps up to the pulpit. He is the polar opposite to his wife—subdued to her eccentric. I think that's what makes them work. He's the reason behind her chaos—the quiet to her loud. Together, they work as a team.

"Thank you all for coming today," he warbles. "It's a good day in the house of the Lord."

A chorus of Amens follows his greeting. I lean forward, putting my elbows on my knees—my hands clasped together.

"There's been a message on my heart all week," Pastor Evert says. "It wasn't part of my original plan for the sermon, but when God leads you to something, I've found that you better listen."

He waits a moment, running his hands along the edge of the pulpit.

"The first sermon I ever remember listening to as a boy was about the woman at the well. As a child, the concept didn't quite stick with me, but as an adult, I think it's one we all need to remember, especially myself," he says. "There's no need to raise your hands, but I want you to think about something. How many of you feel unworthy of the life you were given?"

He slips his hand in the air, and several others raise theirs. Mine stay firmly planted in front of me.

"Now, how many of you feel you have to work for that worth?"

A few more hands slip into the air. Mine twitch, but I keep them clasped together.

"Friends, I am here to tell you today that you are already worthy. In John chapter four, John tells us about Jesus's encounter with a woman at the well. By our standards, she also is not worthy. She had five husbands. Can you imagine? My wife can hardly put up with just me."

The congregation lets out a small chuckle—his grin contagious.

"This woman was an adulteress, the least of these. But—and isn't it always the but that makes it worth it? She met Jesus at the well, and it changed her life."

I pull at the collar of my shirt. The cotton was soft this morning when I put it on, but now it's like sandpaper against my skin. Pastor Evert makes eye contact with me and then looks away. I can't help feeling like I'm being called out.

"Society tells us that we are failures because of our mistakes. It feels like we can never live up to God's grace, but the word of God tells us that we are enough despite our mistakes. The Savior of the world sat down with this woman who, by society's terms, was an outcast, but he offered her living water despite that. He offered her grace. You, my friend, are also worthy of grace."

My heart thumps in a thundering rhythm as I pull harder at my collar. I've never had this much trouble out of a shirt before.

Mrs. Evert's hand slides up to mine and pulls it away from my shirt.

She leans over and whispers, "He's talking to you, and I don't mean my husband, either."

I throw her a questioning look, but she merely chuckles and pats my hand.

"You just have to open up those ears of yours and listen."

———————

When the sermon is over, I don't stick around to talk to anyone. Emryn's parents head my way, but I'm not in the right head space to hang around and speak with them. I have to get this shirt off.

I slip out of the door and head home.

My dad sits on my front stoop as I pull up my driveway.

I cut the engine and stare at the man who was supposed to be my protector—the betrayal fresh on my mind from reliving my mother's funeral. He failed me in ways I can never imagine failing my daughter.

Today, he's wearing a tattered flannel. Aside from the flannel, he's different from the last time he was here. His hair is cut, and his beard combed. The image of my father put together is jarring.

I jerk hard at the collar of my shirt again. I'm burning it in the firepit when I get it off.

I shove open the truck door—ready to get this conversation over with.

My steps are slow and measured as I approach where he is sitting.

When I stand beside him, he looks up at me, and concern creases his brow.

Irritation flashes across my skin, making it tight. He's concerned now that I'm a grown man who can care for himself—not when I needed him.

"What are you doing here?" I ask.

His weathered hands rub against one another.

"I wanted to check in on you, Son."

Son.

It's a simple word. It should be, anyway. I know he isn't trying to start a fight, but that word causes the back of my neck to prickle.

"Son, huh? Why wasn't I your son when I sat by a graveside, sobbing into another man's arms as they buried my mom? Your sentiments don't mean much here, *Dad*." I spit out the word, leaving a bitter taste in my mouth.

I haven't called him that in years. I never felt the need to. The man at the grocery store who let me take home some of the outdated food before I was old enough to get a job was more of a father than Kip was. At least he made sure I was fed.

His shoulders slump in, and, for a moment, I feel sorry for him. Especially when I consider the message I just listened to, but the problem is that anger is never far behind. My anger towards him has festered like a wound—each time he comes around, that wound is poked and prodded.

"Listen, Brooks, I didn't come here to cause you trouble. I came because I found something that might help you."

"I don't want anything you have to offer," I say, crossing my arms over my chest.

It's harsh but true. I don't want anything from this man. I don't owe him any part of my life. I'm tired of him pretending that I do. I put up with him because of who he is to my daughter. Despite how bad of a dad he was, he is a good grandfather to Avery. I won't take that relationship away from my little girl, but that doesn't mean I'm willing to cultivate my own with him.

A sneer crosses his face, and suddenly, he's the Kip I remember. His clean-cut hair and trimmed-up beard can't hide the annoyance that flicks through his eyes.

"Now boy, don't be stubborn just because I'm the one offering," He jumps up from the stairs and wags his finger at me like he's scolding a child.

I would have cowered in the corner if he had made that move when I was younger. He never hit me, but he was good at intimidation—especially when he'd been drinking.

I don't hide this time. I'm bigger than he is. Years of alcohol abuse have left him frail.

I square my shoulders and stand a little taller.

"I'll remind you, Kip. You are on my property. You can leave at any time."

"Fine," he says, resigned—annoyance leaving his features. A look I've never seen from him replaces it. Defeat, maybe? "I can tell when I'm not wanted, but take this."

He flicks a card in my direction, and I snatch it before it hits the ground.

It's a black card with gold lettering on the front. The name G.L. Inspection stands out. Underneath the company name are the words Grayson Lewis, CEO.

I've heard of this company. Many home buyers used them for our new construction projects while trying to get loans. They're well known, and their owner is a shark. He's a little older than me, and unlike me, he built his company from the ground up and made it successful. Though the rumors are, he's impossible to work for. His company is located three counties over, so I've never met the guy. It's hard to say what rumors are true.

I look from the card to my dad, wondering how he got the card—and why.

"What's this for?" I ask. "In case you haven't noticed, I have a house. I'm not in the market for buying another."

"They're hiring," he states as if the answer should have been obvious, but I'm still stuck on how somebody like Kip would have the owner's card. My dad doesn't scream well-off by looking at him, so it's not like he is their ideal clientele.

"And you know this how?" I ask.

He turns towards the mountain that lines the field beside my house.

"I can't tell you that, not right now, at least."

I scoff, "You can tell me they are hiring, but you can't tell me how you know that?"

He shakes his hand, still not meeting my eyes.

"Then take the card," I say, shoving it back at him. "I don't want to be mixed up with anything you have going on. Let me remind you, Kip, you only get to see my daughter if you stay clean."

He twists towards me—hurt marring his face.

"You think I'm drinking again?"

"I don't know what to think. All I know is that you are being secretive about where you got that card, and based on experience, secrets with you always mean you're into something bad."

He ignores my accusations, reaches up, and wraps his fingers around mine, pushing the card back into my palm.

"Call them. They are expecting your call. But, Brooks—this interview doesn't change who you are. You can stop trying to prove to people that you aren't like me. Everyone already knows you are ten times the man I will ever be. Don't stress yourself to death trying to get out from under my shadow."

He claps his hand against my shoulder, the closest thing to affection I've ever received from him, before he turns and leaves.

Once again, I'm left staring after him.

The collar of my shirt rubs against my neck again. I rip it off, throwing it to the ground.

A mix of emotions run through my chest—worry that Kip is drinking again, guilt for being so tough on him.

I sat in church this morning and listened to Pastor Evert preach about grace, and I just showed my dad none. I don't know how to do that with him, though.

My whole life, he's wanted nothing to do with being a dad to me, but this is twice that he's shown up out of the blue with the intention of helping me.

How do you forgive someone and show them grace when all they have ever shown you is the back of their hand?

A headache forms behind my eyes.

I don't have time for this right now. On my way inside, I swipe the shirt off the ground and pitch it in the fire pit.

The card is in my other hand, and I pause a minute, debating throwing it in the fire too. It flexes and folds between my fingers as I stare at it before finally slipping it into my pocket.

The part of me that's still that broken boy—crying for his mom and waiting for his dad to show up—wants this card to mean something, but the man who recognizes reality realizes that it's more than likely just another way I'm going to be disappointed.

Chapter 16

Brooks

The driveway to Emryn's parent's house winds up the side of a mountain. Nerves settle in my stomach as I take the curves like the daredevil teenage boy I once was. I used to drive up this mountainside at top speed to get to Emryn quicker. It's nice to have that feeling of excitement back again.

One final curve and the house comes into view, a log cabin with windows that take up most of the house. My eyes settle on the wrap-around porch where a lone figure sits on the swing, and I recognize Emryn's dad sitting there.

If I hadn't been feeling like a teenage boy before, I am now.

The week I got my license, I bought a beat-up truck. You could see the ground in parts of the floorboard, but I only gave seven hundred dollars for it. It was mine, and I had bought it on my own. I was proud of that thing. At that point, Emryn and I had been official for a while, but I had never taken her on a proper date. I couldn't afford much, but I loaded up a picnic, jumped in my truck, and made my way to her as fast as possible. When I pulled up in the driveway, Jonathan was sitting on the swing, waiting for me like he is now. He's intimidating, especially considering my father was nothing more than a drunk. When I stepped out of the truck that day, my legs were visibly shaking. He met me on the steps and asked me to sit a while before Emryn came down.

Saying no was not an option. I thought I would get one of those speeches about making sure his daughter made it home safely—all my friends had gotten a version of their own from their girlfriend's dad.

That night, he sat me down and asked about my life. He was interested in knowing me and my future, not because I was dating his daughter, but because he was interested in me.

I'd been around him plenty of times, but aside from the day of my mother's funeral, I'd never let him get too close. This was the first time I let him get to know me.

Because of my dad, I had always found Jonathan off-putting. I couldn't understand his sincerity. That night, though, I wanted him to trust me to take his daughter out, so I let him in. Looking back, I can honestly say that decision saved my life. He filled a gap my dad couldn't.

When I pull to a stop and round the corner of my pickup, just like that day twelve years ago, he rises off the swing and meets me on the steps.

The words that leave his mouth when I'm standing on the stairs below him nearly have my knees buckling out from under me.

"I'm proud of you."

Sincerity shines from his eyes, and I have to clear the emotion out of my throat before responding.

"What for, sir?" I ask.

He studies me a moment before he claps me on the back and says, "You're trying, and that's all anyone can ask for. Come on. Let's sit a minute before you leave."

He sits back on the swing, and I take the rocking chair next to it.

As I rock, I can hear Emryn inside chasing Avery. I breathe in the fresh air, the chill nipping at my nose. Giggles float outside through the open windows, and contentment fills my soul.

Nothing else matters—not my job status or the multiple phone calls

I've gotten from my dad—nothing.

"Brooks," Jonathan starts. "I would like to discuss something with you, and I'm going to ask that you keep an open mind."

A feeling of unease in my stomach threatens the peace surrounding me.

"I'll try, sir."

The swing rocks back and forth as he takes his time to respond. I scratch at the scruff on my jawline as I try and fail not to fidget.

"I know you would never ask this," he starts, "You're stubborn, and I recognize there is a reason for your pride. Your circumstances were hard growing up, and, as a man, you want to prove you are better than that. Before I go on, I want you to know you already have. You are more than those circumstances. But, here's the thing, Brooks— sometimes, we have to see past our pride and recognize that we also need help. Accepting help doesn't make you less of a man, so if you are interested—a job is waiting for you with my company."

I have a lot of respect for the man in front of me. There has never been a day he hasn't been there for his family. I want to take what he is offering, but a part of me still struggles to rely on anyone other than myself.

"What kind of job?" I ask. I hate myself for even asking—for letting it be a possibility I will consider, but he's right. I'm not having any luck finding a job, and if it comes down to it, I will put my pride aside for my family.

"I'm looking for an ambassador for my road construction contract. We are working with the state to build a new highway and update some older ones. You would be the correspondence point for that."

I wished it had been any other job. If he had asked me to run some of the machinery, I wouldn't have hesitated to take him up on the offer, but I can't do this for him. I managed my business into the ground, and he's offering to put a major project for his company in my hands.

What if I fail like I did with mine? I can't do that to him.

"Can I think about it?" I ask.

He nods, "It's waiting for you when you're ready."

I don't respond— I don't need to. We sit and rock in silence until the front door creaks open, and Emryn and Avery step out.

My heart stutters in my chest at the sight of my girls together. I miss them.

A squeal comes from Avery when she sees me, and she runs to me, jumping in my lap.

"Daddy," she yells, throwing her arms around my neck.

"Hi, sweetheart. I missed you."

"I missed you too. Mommy says you're going on a date. Can I come?"

"Not today. You're going to stay with Grandma and Grandpa. Maybe next time, okay?"

She shrugs, not putting up a fight. Why would she when it means she gets to stay here and be spoiled rotten by her grandparents?

"Okay, Daddy," she pauses and leans close to whisper the next part conspiratorially, "But if you're going on a date with Mommy, you're 'opposed to bring her flowers. It's the rule."

I press my lips together, trying not to laugh because her whisper is as subtle as a bomb. She might as well have been yelling it to Jesus. I glance over her head at Emryn, who is holding back her own laugh.

Without breaking eye contact with Emryn, I whisper in Avery's ear loud enough for her momma to hear, "Why don't you go check the truck? I think I might have remembered the rule."

A smile lights up Avery's face as she hops off my lap and takes off running to the truck. She won't be able to open the door, so I amble along behind her.

She's bouncing from one foot to the other as I make my way to her. Before I have the door fully open, she climbs inside and grabs the sunflowers on the passenger seat.

122

CHAPTER 16

Once on the ground, she crooks her finger at me, beckoning me to lean down to her level. I crouch down so we are face to face.

"Good work, Daddy," she says as she pats my face. "Now, go give these to Mommy."

This time, I let out a soft chuckle. Taking the flowers from her little hand, I pull one out of the dozen and hand it to her.

"You remember this when you are older and get a boyfriend of your own." I wink.

Her giggle is like music to my ears as I pick her up and carry her back to the porch. I stop in front of Emryn and hand her the rest of the bouquet.

Tears brim her eyes as she stares at it, and from the smile on her face, I know I've gotten it right this time.

"Thank you," she mouths, and I wonder how I could have ever forgotten what it was like to see this type of happiness in her eyes.

——————————

As we leave the house, my palms are sweaty, leaving streaks on my steering wheel. I wipe them against my jeans, hoping Emryn doesn't notice.

She's sitting in the passenger seat—too far away from me. I want to reach across the seat and pull her closer, but I'm not sure how she will react. So, instead, I tighten my hands on the steering wheel and throw glances her way every few minutes, trying to gauge her thoughts.

Not for the first time—I wish I was a mind reader. Maybe then things would have been easier in our marriage.

My eyes slide to her again. This time, when my eyes meet hers, there's determination on her face.

I can see it in the purse of her lips and glint in her eyes. It makes me wary of her next move.

I flick my eyes back to the road but keep an eye on her in my peripheral. After a deep breath and a sharp nod, she's sliding across

123

the bench seat until the outside of her thigh brushes mine.

My breath hitches, and I fight to keep my breathing steady.

"Well, hello, darling," I smirk, slipping an arm around her shoulders.

One move from her and the nerves that are like a noose around my throat suddenly loosen.

A smile plays on her lips and lights up her whole face.

I will do anything to keep it there for the rest of our lives.

She lays her head on my shoulder and whispers into the fabric of my flannel, "I've missed you."

It's the exact words I whispered to her at the park, and it does something to my gut to hear her say them to me now.

I've missed her too. I've missed the weight of her head on my shoulder as I drive and the feeling of contentment that settles in my chest when she's near.

I place a soft kiss on top of her hair and pull her tighter against me.

"Where are we going?" she asks.

"I could tell you," I quip, "but then I'd have to kill you. It's top secret."

Her elbow digs into my hip, and I yelp as if she's actually wounded me.

She shakes her head against my shoulder, mocking my theatrics.

"Come on, just give me a hint," she pleads.

I shake my head. "Not a chance."

Crossing her arms and huffing, she leans away, but I'm faster. I pull her against me and whisper against her hair, "It's been a long time since I've held you. I'm not letting go of you so soon."

She nuzzles in closer to me and flicks the radio on—humming off-key to each song that comes on.

The rest of the drive takes fifteen minutes. I slow my truck down as a dirt road comes into view. It's one we've driven down a hundred times over the years, worn and bumpy.

As we come to a complete stop, I take my arm from around her shoulders to put the truck in four-wheel drive. Emryn glances out the window and then back at me.

"What are we doing here?" she asks.

"You'll see. Hang on tight."

She giggles as I hit ruts that send her careening into me. I might hit a couple extra just to keep her close.

When we reach the clearing that leads to the banks of the lake, I put the truck in park and turn towards her. She's not looking at me. Instead, she's staring off into the distance where, in a grove of trees, there's a small table set up—complete with a cowhide thrown over the top for a tablecloth, candles in the middle, and a picnic basket beside the two chairs.

Her hand flies to her mouth as she takes it all in.

"Did you do this?" she asks.

I reach out and cup her face in my palms, turning it until she is looking at me.

"I see you, Emryn. I might have missed what you needed from me before, but I won't let that happen again."

Tears, like diamonds, glimmer on her eyelashes. Leaning in, she searches my face, looking for permission I will never deny her. Her lips brush against mine for only a second—a tease, and then she's gone.

Grabbing my hand, she races off to the picnic, and I follow her like a lost puppy finding his way home.

When we reach the table, I grab the picnic basket off the ground and open it up.

I rub the back of my neck, nerves billowing in my stomach.

"I—uh—just want you to know the food isn't much. I just hope you remember."

Her eyelashes drop as she eyes me suspiciously. I reach into the basket and pull out each item I packed—first the peanut butter, then the jelly, and finally the bread.

My eyes rest on her as she takes it all in.

I could have brought a fancy dinner—I even contemplated it—but this is where we started.

I was flat broke growing up. I couldn't afford to take her on fancy dates, so most of the time, we came to the lake banks and ate peanut butter and jelly sandwiches. I know we are trying to figure out this new, grown-up version of ourselves together, but I think that version must also be interwoven with where we've come from.

She places her hand on my chest, right over my heart. The *thump, thump, thump* resounding against her fingertips.

"I remember, Brooks. Those days were important to me too, so thank you. For all of this."

I bow my head, the words getting stuck against the knot in my throat before I clear it. "Let's eat."

My dad might not have been around much, but my momma taught me to be a gentleman. I pull out Emryn's seat, waiting for her to sit. Once she is comfortable, I take my seat.

Pulling out the bread and knife, I spread the peanut butter on a sandwich for my wife.

I can feel Emryn's eyes watching me—tracking my movements. Electric shocks prickle my skin at each place her eyes touch. It's a test of my patience to keep my focus on the sandwich when I want to pick her up and kiss her until she remembers what it's like to be loved by me.

"I'm sorry I walked out, Brooks."

I hold my breath, letting it burn in my lungs before releasing it.

I've come to terms with the fact that my actions drove her away, but I can't say that I haven't been angry at her for leaving.

I understand why she needed to leave. She needed things I wasn't giving her, and I was too stubborn to realize how broken we were.

The problem is, I needed something from her too.

126

She walked out, and I needed her to stay—to prove her love wasn't conditional.

"You made the choice that you thought was best for you—and our daughter. We both needed to change, so you aren't the only one who needs to apologize. I'm sorry for letting our marriage slip to the bottom of my priority list."

"I forgive you, Brooks."

"For what it's worth," I say, "I forgive you too. I can't say that forgiveness was easy, though."

She jerks her head in agreement, but I don't think she understands. How could she when I haven't told her?

"When I was little," I start, "until the day my mom died, my dad was in and out of my life. Even on the days he did manage to come home, he was usually drunk and mean. I never knew what a stable family looked like until I met you. You've been around me long enough to know all that. What you don't know, though, is that when you left, all I could think about was how my love was never enough to make people stay—that maybe I'm the reason people leave."

She opens her mouth, but I interrupt. I have to get this out. It's not easy for me to lay myself open, but I'll do it—for us.

"I recognize that part of that's true. I *was* part of the problem with us, Emryn, but I also trusted you to be there when I was falling apart. I should have told you about work, and I would have, but somewhere along the way, it started to feel like my mess was too much for you. So—I kept it to myself because I was terrified of you leaving when you found out how much of a screw-up I am. Then you left anyway."

Tears slide down her cheeks, and I reach to brush them away. I hate that I'm hurting her, but if I've learned anything from this, it's that we have to be honest with each other.

"I didn't know how else to get you to see that we were struggling," she says, head tilted down, staring at the table. "I should have tried harder."

"We both should have."

She wipes the back of her hand against her cheek to remove the last evidence of her tears.

"You know what?" I ask. "This is a date. It's supposed to be fun—no more tears."

She bobs her head in agreement as I pick up the abandoned food and finish making our meal.

Chapter 17

Emryn

I t's been a long time since I've eaten a peanut butter and jelly
sandwich. At some point, sandwiches became home-cooked
meals and table settings. Today makes me realize that some days
can be a PB&J day.

The simplicity of this moment settles in my soul. My heart has been
craving this feeling for months. It's peaceful.

"Penny for your thoughts?" Brooks's deep voice breaks into my
musings. When the chill of the October sky cut into my bones, he built
us a fire. Now we are wrapped in a blanket, lying next to the water's
edge and letting the flames warm us.

A million stars dot the sky, giving just enough light to make out the
shadow of Brooks's face when I look up at him. I let my hand drift up
to his jaw, caressing the stubble there.

"I was thinking that I'm happy I took the chance on this date. I was
scared, but this has been the best night I've had in a long time."

He tilts his head down and places a kiss against my hairline.

"Me too."

His hand floats in circles against the small of my back. I sigh.

"Tell me something you dream about, Brooks."

It's time I learn who my husband is again. Biggest dreams and
slightest fears—I want to know it all.

"You're my dream," he states.

"Oh, come on—be for real."

His hand stops moving on my back, and he sits up, gently pulling me with him. We are face to face—breaths mingling as one. The callouses on his palm rub against my cheek as he cups my face. I lean into his embrace, relishing the feel of it.

"I am for real, Emryn. Come on," he says. He drops his hand from my face, and I immediately miss the warmth. Grabbing my hand, he helps me stand, and I follow as he drags me to a cluster of trees behind where the table is.

He stops in front of one tree that's twisted at the bottom.

"Look," he says, pulling his phone out of his pocket and pointing the flashlight at its base.

It's hard to see, so I have to scoot closer to see what he's pointing at.

There, at the base, our initials are carved out, and a heart surrounds them.

I remember the day he carved this.

It was his seventeenth birthday. His mom was gone, and his dad never remembered. My family always tried to heal the pieces of him that his family had broken, so that day, we had a surprise party for him at our house. My dad had wrapped up the pocket knife he always carried around and gifted it to Brooks.

He cherished that thing—I think mostly because it was my dad's.

After the party, we drove out here to watch the sunset. While we waited, he took the knife out of his pocket and carved our names. Then he turned to me and told me he would marry me for real someday.

He pulls at the tip of my hair until I pull my eyes away from the tree and look at him, "You are my dream. You have been since I was six years old, and I watched you beat up Kota Miller for being mean to a girl in the grade below us."

Laughter bubbles out of me at the memory. My shoulders rise and then fall. I refuse to apologize for that particular situation—even if I did end up suspended for one day.

"Kota Miller was a bully. Someone needed to stand up to him."

He chuckles and drops a kiss on my forehead, "You always have been my hero."

I roll my eyes and shove at his chest, pushing him away from me, but he's too quick. He catches my hand and laces our fingers. I don't fight against it. I let his fingers wrap around mine like a tether to him.

Hand in hand, we walk back to the fire. He sits and pulls me into his lap, wrapping the blanket around us. I lay my head on his shoulder—against the crook of his neck— and his arms tighten around me.

"I told you my dream," he says, his voice intimate against my hair. "Now you tell me yours. What do you dream about, Emryn?"

"I dream about you, Brooks," I say, my lips brushing against the skin that peeks out above the collar of his flannel with each word.

A shiver runs down his spine, and I smile against his neck.

"You're trying to distract me, but I'm not going to let you," Brooks says, his voice rumbling deep inside his chest. "It's okay to have dreams outside of me—as long as I can be a part of them. I stood by and watched as you lost a little bit of yourself in being my wife and Avery's mom, and I was too dense to realize it until you pointed it out. I want you to find that piece again. I should have never let you lose it to begin with."

I close my eyes and let his scent—a mix of outdoors and spice—wash over me.

He will always be a part of my dream, but I *have* lost a piece of me. I'm slowly starting to find it, though, and it's nice to know that he will support me as I do.

"I told you I have been subbing and applied for school. It's been a long time since I've been in school, and I wasn't sure if I wanted to continue down the education route or go a different direction. Subbing has put that in perspective."

"And?" he asks. "What did you decide?"

"I love being in the classroom—watching the light bulb flip on in a kid's brain when they understand. I'm passionate about it, and that passion is what I've been missing."

"Then I think you should go for it, and I'll be behind you, cheering you on. Heck, I'll carry you to the finish line if you need me to—whatever you need from me."

"You know I'll do the same for you, right?" I ask.

He squirms beneath me.

"Can you talk about your job?" I prod.

"What about my job?" he asks briskly, the softness of his body turning rigid beneath me.

And, just like that, this conversation careens two steps back, but if Brooks wants us to move forward, he has to learn to share the parts of himself he wants to keep hidden.

"What do you want to do now that the company is gone?"

"Haven't given it a lot of thought."

His answer is short—blunt, rigid. That peace from moments ago settles like a rock in my belly.

"Okay, you know what, never mind," I clamber off his lap, gathering our stuff and turning my back to him.

My movements are jerky and harsh, but it's the only way I won't cry. I don't notice Brooks slip behind me until his arms circle my waist. I try to push them off. I can't take him touching me right now.

"Hey," he whispers. "Come here. I'm sorry."

A few stray tears escape, and I brush them away with the palm of my hand.

My back is still to him, but I let him pull me against him. His chest pushes against my back, warding off the chill that permeates the air.

"I need you to try," I beg.

"I know. I *am* sorry, Emryn. It's just—hard for me to talk about. I feel like I failed you and Avery."

I turn in his arms and allow him to see the tears slipping down my cheeks.

"You didn't fail us, Brooks. Life happens, and that stinks, but you didn't fail us. Failing us would mean that you gave up. Have you given up?"

"Well, no, but—"

"No buts," I reply. "Don't push me out this time. *Please.* Let me be your safe space. You can tell me anything, and I won't think less of you, okay?"

He places his chin on top of my head and nods.

"Your dad offered me a job," he says eventually.

"Are you going to take it?"

"Do you want me to?"

"Brooks," I say. "This isn't about me. This is a decision you have to make for you. I want to be here to support you—to help you talk it through—but you have to follow your heart here. Otherwise, you will end up lost like I was."

"I don't know what I want."

"And that's okay, but can you promise to talk to me when you do?" I ask.

His arms squeeze tight around me when he says, "I promise."

Our progress is slow, but it's progress.

The crickets and frogs sing around us, creating a symphony as he holds me.

I could stay here all night, but I know we have to leave soon.

Avery is waiting for us. We are like teenagers with a curfew, except this time, it's our daughter laying down the rules.

It doesn't stop me from wanting to stay in this moment just a little longer, though. Because the truth is, I'm not sure what comes next.

I'm terrified of what will happen after we leave this bubble tonight. We still have a lot of things to work on, but for once, we are heading in the right direction. Brooks opened up to me tonight. I took for granted how much his childhood affected him, and I hate that I made him question his worth.

I can't help but wonder if it's time I go home. I've asked for effort from him, and he's given me that. It's time I give him what he needs from this marriage.

I don't want him to believe that my love is conditional on him meeting all my needs and getting nothing in return—it's not.

He deserves my effort.

I moved out to protect Avery, but I have to question whether that's what I'm doing now.

Am I dragging my feet to return to protect her heart, or am I trying to save mine?

Dr. Phelps made a comment at our session last week that's stuck with me.

At the end of the session, after Brooks and I were both wrung out emotionally, Dr. Phelps looked at us and said, "We can either protect ourselves, or we can open up and give someone else a chance to protect us. But—only one of those options comes with love."

He might have been talking to both of us, but what he said hit me like lightning. It was God opening my eyes to where my path is leading, and I've been resistant to it all week.

I've been in denial. Not because I don't want to go home, but because I'm scared too.

What he said makes sense now. I can't shield myself from Brooks and let him love me simultaneously. If I want us to work, I have to act like we will work. I can't hug the edge of a cliff, waiting for the mountain to crumble—sending us into a free fall.

I tilt my head up to look at Brooks. It's nice to see him without stress

134

lining the corner of his eyes. A few months ago, I wasn't sure we would have a moment like this again. Now, here we are, still with a lot of problems to fix, but at least with a way forward.

"I want to come home."

His eyes search mine. The moment stretches out without him saying anything—an uneasiness forms in my stomach.

Maybe he thinks it's too soon—that I'm rushing it after only one date.

I've loved him my whole life. We hit a rough spot, and I needed space. But—I never planned for that space to be permanent. In a way, it was selfish of me to leave, but I didn't know how else to fix us.

Now I have a better idea, and it's time I go home. Brooks still hasn't said anything, but I'm ready to fight him on this—to fight for us, but I don't have to.

"I would like you to come home too," he says. His voice is gravelly as he runs his hand through my hair.

When he presses his lips against my temple, I know home will always be with him.

"You dirty dog," Mia yells, bursting into the third-grade classroom I'm subbing for.

Luckily, they are at art.

"Well, hello to you too, Mia."

"Don't you sass me," she says, wagging her finger in front of my nose. "You went on a date with your hunky husband and didn't tell me."

Since the day Mia invited me to dinner, we've been getting closer. She's the first friend, outside of Brooks, I remember having.

"Mia, that's my husband you're talking about. Plus, you have a boyfriend. I don't think you can call Brooks hunky. Also, how did you find out about the date?"

Her nose crinkles at the mention of her boyfriend. From my

135

understanding, she and Chase have been together for two years, but I don't think they are in a good place—not that she's said that. She claims they are happier than ever, but her body language tells a different story. Waving a hand, she dismisses me. "I may be new to town, but nothing is a secret here. The hunkiness is an objective observation. Now, tell me about the date."

Plopping into a chair beside me, she places her elbow on the desk and props her chin in her hand—waiting for the details.

"It was nice," I say, turning my head so she can't see the heat burning my cheeks.

Mia's sitting position doesn't last long. She bursts up, knocking the container of pens over. "Nice? That's all I get is nice?" she asks. Her expression turns serious, and her hand flies to her mouth. "Was it secretly awful? Oh, it was, and here I am demanding the details."

Mia would ramble on all day if I let her. The girl likes to talk, but she's genuine. I've needed someone in my life like that. She is twenty-two to my twenty-eight—only a couple of years out of college—so sometimes, it feels strange that she's becoming one of my best friends. We are in different stages of life, but I think God knew I needed a Mia.

Her rambling turns into single phrases—like shovel and pig, and I know it's time I step in. "Mia, I'm moving back home."

"WHAT?" she screams. "Why didn't you lead with that? Nice, you said. I think it was a little more than 'nice.' Tell. Me. Everything."

"Okay," I giggle, "but you have to sit down and listen."

She mimes zipping her lips, and plops down in one of the bean bag chairs on the reading carpet.

"When we were teenagers, we always had this spot at the lake we would go to. It's been a long time since we've been there—I had almost forgotten about it. After he picked me up, he wouldn't tell me where we were going. When we pulled up to the trail that leads back to the lake, those memories of being young and carefree came flooding back.

Then, once we were back there, he had a picnic set up—with a romantic table and everything."

Mia feigns swooning—closing her eyes, placing her hand against her forehead, and falling back against the other beanbags. She peeks one eye open and says, "Did he cook? Please tell me he cooked."

I shoot her a shy smile, chewing on my bottom lip as I think about the thought Brooks put into this date. "He made peanut butter and jelly sandwiches."

She shakes her head. "I'm sorry, what?"

"It's kind of our thing," I say, picking at the hem of my skirt.

Her grin as she stares at me is contagious. Pretty soon, my cheeks ache from smiling.

"In all seriousness," Mia says, "I'm happy for you. I know we haven't known each other long, Emryn, but you are a good person. And—from what I can tell, Brooks is a good guy that got a little lost."

"I was a little lost, but thanks for dragging me out of my car that first day of subbing, Mia. It put me in a place where I could find myself— and I think that's the part that will save my marriage the most. I know who I am now, and I won't let myself get lost again. Brooks and I still have a lot to work on, but I feel more confident that we can."

"I'm glad, Emryn. Do you need help moving back?" she asks.

"No," I say, shaking my head. "It's mostly just mine and Avery's clothes. I can handle that, but why don't we have a cookout at our house once we are settled? I would love for you to meet Brooks in person, and you can bring your boyfriend. I want to meet him too. I'll even invite my family. We can make it a whole thing."

She smiles, but the brightness of it doesn't quite meet her eyes, "I would love that—just tell me when."

Chapter 18

Emryn,
  Today's the day you come home to me, and I feel like a kid on Christmas morning. It's early morning as I write this, but I can't sleep. I keep staring at this paper, smiling like a love-sick boy. I've never been one for words, but maybe if I write down all the thoughts running through my head, I can sleep a little.

Since the day you left, this house has been soulless. I miss the sounds that used to fill my morning—Avery's giggles, the way you sigh when you take your first sip of tea, all of it.

You are the heart of this family. I need you to know that. I'm sorry it took you leaving for me to recognize what I was missing before. Things are going to change. I am going to change. I promise.

When we got married, I vowed a lot of things to you, but I let you down. I was a young kid who didn't understand the promises a man makes to his wife. I just knew that I loved you, and I would have done anything to make you happy. So, before you come back home, I want to make some promises to you.

I promise to always hold your hand when you sit beside me in my truck. Better yet, I promise to pull you close to my side so I can feel your heartbeat against me.

When you walk into a room, I promise to notice if you cut your hair, and I'll even tell you I noticed.

138

Each time we fight, I'll grab the ice cream if you get the hot fudge. Keeping both those things in our kitchen is another thing I'll need to add to the list of promises.

I'll make good on that promise as soon as the store opens this morning.

More than any of the others, I promise to work on my communication with you.

I know these are all just words. They mean nothing without action, but I won't lose you again. It hurt too much watching you walk out the door the first time.

I wasn't sure I would ever be able to breathe again. There's been a hole in my chest since that day, and it finally feels like it's starting to heal.

I didn't grow up in a home full of love like you. I know my upbringing wasn't my fault, but it left its mark. No one taught me how to love you. I know Momma would have, but she left me before she could. Her death and all the things I had to deal with after created an insecurity I didn't know I had until you were gone too. I let my past dictate my future, but no more.

I'm not saying that insecurity will be gone in a day because it won't. I will work on it, though, and that's all I can give you. I hope it's enough.

You deserve to be loved properly. Our daughter deserves to see that.

I want to love you so well that Avery never has to question what love looks like. When she gets older, I want her to know her worth because of how I love you.

All of this is to say that I will mess up sometimes. We might fight, but I will never let you walk out the door again without me following.

Love you always,

Brooks

Chapter 19

Emryn

Avery's quiet as we pull out of the drive of my parents' home. She's going to miss seeing them every day. They've spoiled her rotten.

"Are you excited to go home and see Daddy?" I ask.

Her lip, which had been poking out moments before, tugs into a smile at the mention of her daddy. I may have gotten a lot of things wrong in this life, but choosing the father of my child is not one of them. The man adores our little girl.

"Daddy said we could go pick flowers for you in the field. It's supposed to be a secret, so don't tell."

I press my lips together. The girl couldn't keep a secret if she tried. I debated making Mom and Dad's anniversary party a surprise, but there's no way they wouldn't have found out through Avery. I opted for something a little more formal instead. They love to get dressed up and dance, and I want it to be special for them. Plus, I found a way to have a surprise for them anyway—one that no one besides Tayte knows about.

I zip my lips, locking it and throwing away the key.

"My lips are sealed," I mumble around my closed lips.

Giggles erupt from the back seat, warming my heart.

It's been a few days since I saw Brooks, but we've talked on the phone

140

every day. Now, my car is loaded up, and Avery and I are heading home. I'm ready to sleep in my bed—next to my husband.

It's a five-minute drive to my house from my parents. When we pull into the drive, Brooks stands on the porch waiting for us.

The man is too handsome for his own good. His arms are crossed over his broad chest, and one shoulder is propped up against the porch post—hat flipped backward.

I forget my name for a second.

"Uh– Mommy? Why are we stopped in the middle of the driveway?" Avery asks.

I blink myself out of my stupor and look around. Heat fills my cheeks because she's right. I stopped in the middle of the driveway to ogle my husband.

Brooks breaks out into laughter on the porch. He's bent over with one hand on his knee and the other clutching his stomach.

I roll my eyes and finish pulling into the rest of the drive, stopping just outside of the garage.

By the time I've pulled to a stop, Brooks has managed to collect himself.

He jumps over the front steps, not bothering to take a single one, and is at my door within seconds. Before I can grab the handle, he slings it open, and then he's in my bubble, smelling intoxicating and taking over all my senses.

"You know, driving while distracted is dangerous," he whispers as his lips skim across mine. Mischief sparkles in his eyes, but underneath, there's genuine happiness.

"Well, you shouldn't be so distracting then," I say, pushing on his chest so he gives me enough room to step out of the car.

Taking hold of my arms, he pulls me up—crushing me to his chest.

He's hugged me plenty of times before, but this one is different. There's a desperation in how his arms flex against my back as if I might run if he lets go.

I tilt my chin so I'm looking up at him. A dimple pokes in on his cheek as he smiles down at me. He dips his head and presses his lips against my forehead, and I close my eyes to savor the feel of him.

"Hello, can I get out now?" Avery squeals from her car seat.

I chuckle at her impatience. I would say she gets it from her daddy, but I wouldn't be telling the truth.

"I'm coming. I'm coming. Hold your horses," Brooks grumbles, slinging his arm around my shoulder and leading us to the other side of the car.

Opening the door, he unfastens her seat belt and grabs her up in a bear hug. She giggles and places her hand on each side of his face, smashing his cheeks together.

"I've missed you, Daddy. I'm glad you're out of time out," she pauses, leaning in conspiratorially. "I bet it was the flowers. We should pick some more. Don't tell Mommy, though."

She glances at me to see if I'm watching, and I avert my eyes to pretend I didn't hear her *secret*. When satisfied I didn't hear, she looks back at Brooks and worms out of his arms.

"Come on, Daddy. We're on a mission." She drags him away as he looks back over his shoulder at me, blowing me a dramatic kiss as they head towards the field beside our house.

I watch them a minute longer before I turn and head inside. When I open the door, the sight causes me to pause. I don't know why, but I expected the house to be in disarray. I know it was clean the last time I was here, but I expected it to be a fluke. Maybe it's because I was always the one to take care of the housework when I was here, but everything is spotless when I look down the foyer to the living room and kitchen. There's even a candle lit on the coffee table.

My eyes sting as I blink back the tears.

We are going to be okay.

Our marriage is going to work.

————————————

By the time Avery and Brooks return from the field, I've managed to unload most of our bags and put them in our rooms. I'm unpacking when they slip into my closet, bare feet sliding against the carpet and a huge bouquet of wildflowers in Brooks's hand.

"Look what we got for you, Mommy. Are you surprised?" Avery asks, slinging her arms around my neck.

"Oh, I'm so surprised. They are beautiful, Sweet Girl. Thank you."

"You're welcome. I'm going to go play now," she says, bopping my nose with her finger and flouncing off.

Brooks stands leaning against the door frame, watching me. One arm is above his head, and my mouth goes a little dry. He's watching me with an expression that I can't quite read.

"What?" I ask, looking down at my clothes to make sure I didn't put my shirt on inside out or something.

"Nothing. I'm just enjoying the view," he smirks.

I hum in response. When he tries, the man knows how to make me feel seen.

"Well, don't just stand there staring. Grab a hanger and help," I say, throwing a shirt at him.

He's quick and snatches it out of mid-air.

The smile on his face is nice. He's happy.

"I'll make you a deal," he says, "Come sit with me in the kitchen while I make dinner, and then I'll help you put all this stuff away. Okay?"

"You're cooking?" I ask skeptically. The man burns water.

He throws his head back and laughs. It's a deep, booming laugh that gives me goosebumps all the way down to my toes.

"I guess you'll have to see," he says, crooking his finger for me to follow.

When we reach the kitchen, he grabs my hips, lifts me, and sits me on the counter beside the stove.

"You sit tight and watch the master at work."

"The master, you say?" I ask, crossing my arms. "When did this happen? Because I'm not going to lie, I'm a little scared for my kitchen right now."

He steps closer to the counter, and I wrap my legs around his waist.

"Are you questioning my cooking ability?" he asks, running his nose along my jaw.

I pull back to stare at him.

"Well, I declare, I would never do such a thing," I say, laying the Southern accent on thick to up my innocence.

"I think you would," he says, a dangerous glint in his eyes, "and do you know what happens when you question me?"

I shake my head back and forth—never breaking eye contact.

The corner of his lip tips up, but he doesn't answer with words. He leans down and brushes his lips against mine.

Once. Twice. Three times.

I close my eyes and savor the feel of his lips against mine. The scruff of his beard prickles against my face, guaranteeing I will have beard burn, but I can't bring myself to care. I'm lost in every piece of him— the feel of his flannel bunched up in my hands, the way his hand spans the length of my lower back, pulling me closer to him. It overrides my sense of awareness and leaves me with the need to pull him closer and stay lost in him.

"Mommy, I'm hungry," Avery calls from the stairs.

Brooks takes a step back, putting distance between us and throwing me a wink. I put my cold hands against my heated cheeks to remove some of the flame.

"Come on, turkey," I call. "You can help Daddy cook. Apparently, he's the master now."

She appears in the doorway a moment later, and Brooks picks her up and places her on the counter on the other side of the stove, just like he did me.

"What are we cooking, Daddy?" Avery asks.

Brooks cocks an eyebrow and grins. "My specialty—peanut butter and jelly sandwiches."

I throw my head back and laugh, "That's what the master chef has up his sleeve?"

He has the sense to look a little sheepish before he answers, "You just wait. It will be the best PB&J you've ever eaten."

I slide off the counter and follow him to the pantry, "Teach me your ways then, Master chef."

Chapter 20

Brooks

I sit back in my chair and take in the scene. Emryn sits beside me on a bar stool. Music plays in the background as our daughter chatters over her peanut butter and jelly sandwich.

This is what I've been missing.

Emryn looks up at me and smiles. She's glowing—happiness radiates off of her.

My heart ticked up a beat.

I put my hand out, and she places hers in mine.

Rough against soft.

My hand envelopes hers, pulling her to me. She falls into my lap, and I bury my nose in her hair, breathing in her strawberry scent.

The radio switches to a slow song, one made for dancing.

"Dance with me," I whisper against her hair.

"Right here?" She asks, turning her head and quirking an eyebrow.

"Why not?" I ask, standing and taking her with me until I hold her in my arms, bridal style. Looking at our daughter, I ask, "What do you think, Avery? Should your momma and I dance?"

She claps her hands and giggles, nodding her head in excitement.

"Dance, dance, dance…" she chants around the food shoved in her mouth.

I lower Emryn to the ground, letting her slide down my chest until her feet are a breath from the floor. With my arms wrapped around her back, I begin to sway to the beat of the music.

She smacks me on the back of the head and laughs, "Let me down so we can dance properly, you big oaf."

I grimace and place her feet the rest of the way on the floor

"Easy, Em. We don't need your ninja skills here."

Avery rolls her eyes in perfect timing with Emryn, and I roar with laughter.

I'm in a lot of trouble when that little girl gets older. She's as sassy as her momma.

"Oh, just hush," Emryn says, brushing her hand through the hair at the nape of my neck. Goosebumps pebble my skin—not the most manly reaction, but I'm not ashamed of my response to her. I revel in how her hand skims across my scalp, sending shocks through my system.

"Yes, Ma'am."

For a moment, only the music fills the air. The singer croons, singing about taking the time to notice his girl.

I take those lyrics to heart, noticing Emryn's flushed cheeks as she hums absentmindedly. She's a picture of perfection, with her hair falling out of her ponytail and framing her face.

Wild and happy.

I bring my face so we are cheek to cheek, and I sing against the shell of her ear.

When the song ends, I graze my lips across her skin until they are a millimeter away from her own. I press a kiss against the corner. She closes her eyes, and her breath hitches in her throat.

"I love you, you know," I murmur.

Her eyes snap open, searching mine for any hint that I'm lying. She won't find any. I may have lost sight of it, but I never stopped loving her.

I eye her carefully. I don't expect her to respond. It's not why I said it. I don't want her to go another day questioning how I feel about her. There have been too many days that she's had to wonder already.

A war crosses her features. I understand if she is still conflicted about her feelings. We have a lot to work out. I won't pressure her into examining those feelings before she's ready.

She opens her mouth to respond, but I stop her before she can, "Don't—not right now. I can see the war that's waging in that pretty brain of yours. Don't just say it because I am—take you're time because I'm not going anywhere. I'll earn that love from you again."

Sadness that I don't understand twinkles in her eye. Then she blinks, and it's gone. She places her head on my chest, and we continue to sway even when the song speeds up.

"Come to church with me tomorrow," I say, spinning her out and back into me.

"You've been going to church?" The surprise in her tone stings a little.

If I let it, the question might feel accusatory because it wasn't that long ago that Emryn used to drag me to church every time we went. It wasn't because I didn't want to be there, but I had a business I was trying to grow—a family I had to care for. There were a hundred other things that needed to be done. Emryn got tired of me pleading busyness and stopped asking me to go. Then, after a while, she stopped going too. As far as I know, she hasn't been back. I've been every Sunday since Pastor Evert preached at the woman at the well, and I haven't seen Emryn sitting in the pews with her mom and dad.

It has been my biggest failure as a husband and father—and I've had a lot of them. I should have pushed us to be in church. I should have led my family like I was supposed to. I could blame my failure on my upbringing, but that wouldn't be true. I had Emryn's dad to show me another path. Instead of choosing that path, I chose busyness over trusting that God could grow my business without sacrificing my time with Him.

I'm fixing that now. I want to sit in the pew with my family by my side.

"I have. But I would like you guys there with me. I'm tired of going alone."

She sucks in the side of her cheek, chewing on it—considering me. Then she says, "I would love that."

I drag her closer, picking up the speed of our dancing, and she laughs.

Avery hops down from her seat and meets us on the other side of the bar. She's tapping her foot to her own beat and wiggling her shoulders. I grab her hand and Emryn's and spin them both around. The dancing continues until bedtime, but the lightness in my soul lasts far longer than that.

"Daddy," Avery says as I'm tucking her into bed later that night.

"Yes, turkey?"

"Did you miss tucking me in?"

I nudge her over so I can sit beside her on the bed. Wrapping my arms around her, I say, "Of course I missed it. It's my favorite part of the day."

She considers this, tilting her head and fiddling with her blanket.

"What about Mommy? Did you miss tucking her in?" she asks.

A chuckle slips out, and I pull her closer, squeezing her against me.

"Yes, I missed tucking Mommy in too."

Her head bobs in a short nod. "Good because Mommy missed you too. I think she was scared of the dark because sometimes I could hear her crying in her room. Now you will be able to protect her from monsters."

Pain stabs me directly in the chest. I keep learning new ways I've messed up. I don't know if I'll ever be able to make up for them all, but

I will spend every day until my last breath trying to.

I plant a kiss on the top of Avery's head and stand up to pull the covers up around her.

"Sleep tight, turkey. I love you."

"I love you too, Daddy."

I flip off the light switch and turn on her night light. Blowing her one last kiss, I close the door and leave the room.

Her room is directly across from mine and Emryn's. The door to our room is closed. I hesitate to turn the knob and walk in.

What if Emryn still needs a little space? I know she moved home, but maybe she isn't ready to share the same bed yet—not with all we have to work on still. I've been sleeping on the couch since she left. If she isn't comfortable sharing a bed with me yet, I'll take the couch, but I can't imagine I'll get any sleep with my wife sleeping in our bed alone.

Drawing a deep breath, I let it out as I turn the doorknob.

Emryn's already lying in bed. Her back is towards the door, but she turns her head when she hears me. Red blooms across her cheeks as I stand in the doorway.

I prop my shoulder against the jamb and stand there, appreciating my wife.

She's beautiful. Her face is free of any traces of makeup, making her green eyes brighter. Her hair has gotten longer, and the strawberry blond locks fall over her shoulder.

"Hi," she squeaks.

"Hi." My voice is gravelly—dark—giving away my thoughts. I clear my throat and look out the window. "I can sleep on the couch if you want."

"Oh, okay," she says, turning back to face the wall, and I'm left confused about what I did wrong. I don't want to sleep on the couch, but I want her to be comfortable.

CHAPTER 20

A growl rumbles out of my chest. I surge forward, scoop her up, and place her on my lap as I lay back against the headboard. She lets out a squeak of surprise, burying her face in my chest.

We are not going back this—we've come too far.

"Talk to me, darling," I say, brushing her hair back from her face.

Emryn buries her head deeper into my shirt and mumbles, "Do you not want to sleep with me?"

A harsh laugh slips out, and it's all I can do not to shake this woman until she gets it through her head that she's all I've ever wanted—day and night. Sleeping without her has been torture.

She lifts her head at the sound of my laugh. Her bottom lip is tucked between her teeth. I place my thumb on the bottom and tug to keep her from worrying it.

"That is not the problem, Emryn. I just want you to know I can *keep* sleeping on the couch if you aren't ready to be in the same bed again."

Her brows tug together, creating a crease between them. "What do you mean *keep* sleeping on the couch?"

I turn my head because I didn't mean to admit that.

"I—uh—have been sleeping on the couch since you've been gone. I couldn't stand the thought of sleeping in here without you."

Her fingers are soft as she reaches up and runs them against the scruff of my beard. I don't look back until I feel her push against my jaw, turning my head to her.

"I'm home now. There have been too many nights without you by my side. I refuse to spend any more that way."

"I was hoping you would say that," I say.

I pull her down with me until we are tucked in. Her head lays on my chest, legs thrown over mine. My arm is wrapped around her, hugging her close until we are one. With my chin on top of her head, this feels like home.

151

Chapter 21

Brooks

The following morning is comfortable chaos. The sounds I desperately yearned for are back but with a new tune. Emryn used to take care of the morning routine—picking out Avery's clothes, getting her dressed, and making breakfast—all while I sat in my office and worked. I'm ashamed of that. She shouldn't have had to do that by herself.

That's changing—starting today. I'm learning that our patterns in the past don't have to define our future. We can make different choices when we realize the path we are taking is wrong, and while it's a lesson I needed to learn, it's also one that doesn't sit well with me for other reasons.

For a long time, I've made my dad suffer for the decisions he made while I was growing up, but he's changed—or at least he's trying to.

I've held him captive in the past—holding too tightly to the pain he caused because I was too bitter to recognize that he changed his path. I'm not sure we will ever have the relationship that Emryn has with her dad, but it's time I forgive him—not only for him but for myself.

I can't heal the parts of me that tarnish my marriage if I still let my past control me.

"Penny for your thoughts," Emryn says from behind me, parroting what I asked her on our date, "You seem lost to them this morning."

The stove burns hot in front of me. I'm attempting to make bacon and eggs, but at the sound of her voice, I glance over my shoulder and catch a glimpse of her leaning against the door. In one second flat, I'm turned around, leaning against the counter beside the stove and ogling my wife.

She's breathtaking wearing my T-shirt. The front is doused in water from giving Avery a bath, and the hem hits right above her knee. Her long legs are displayed underneath shorts that peek out just below the t-shirt. Even though summer has faded into fall, she still has a permanent tan. I skate my eyes back up to her lips, studying them like there might be a test later.

She laughs, bringing me out of my reverie, "Well, I guess I don't need to pay a penny for those thoughts. I can practically read your mind."

I shrug, unbothered by getting caught staring, "I can't help that your lips beg to be kissed."

This time, when she laughs, she throws her head back, and my eyes are drawn to the curve of her neck.

This woman is everything I've ever dreamed of. There's never been anyone else that could hold my attention like her.

Reaching over and switching off the stove burner, I take one step towards her—then two. My movements are slow and controlled. I'm on the prowl—ready to press her lips to mine.

Her eyes go wide, watching me as I stalk closer.

At the last second, she darts away, and I savor the chase. She dashes up the stairs with her head start, and I follow leisurely. Soon enough, she'll run out of places to hide, and then she will be mine.

Once I'm up the stairs, I catch up to her as she peeks out the doorway of my office.

"You didn't make it too far," I muse.

"Maybe I was tired of running from you."

"I hope so, pretty girl. I really hope so," I say, pulling her towards me and holding her in my arms.

We stand there for a moment—soaking in each other's presence. It's nice having a morning like this—slow and languid.

"Come on," I say eventually. "I cooked breakfast. We can eat before we go."

Horror fills her features, and she asks, "Is it edible?"

"Ha. Ha. Very funny," I quip.

Stopping by Avery's room, I scoop her up in my arms, and we return to the kitchen.

I grab the food as Emryn grabs the plates—working together like the team we always should have been.

When we finally sit at the table, Avery grabs our hands and looks back and forth—eyes bouncing from mine to Emryn's. A smile flits across her lips.

"Grandpa J says we have to bow our heads and pray before we eat. He said we should pray about everything we are thankful for."

I squeeze her hand, happy that she knows about prayer but also sad that I wasn't the one who taught her.

"He's right. We should do that. Do you want to lead the prayer today since it was your idea?" I ask.

She gives a timid nod before lowering her head. Emryn and I follow suit, but I keep my eyes open, watching Avery. She scrunches her nose up in concentration as she thinks about what she wants to say. Finally, she begins to pray.

"Dear Jesus, I just want to thank you for my mommy and daddy loving each other again. Grandpa J and I have been praying hard for this, ya know. Oh yeah, thanks for letting me sleep in my room again. I like it there. Amen."

She pops her head back up and digs into her food, chattering about her dolls and a tea party she has planned for today while I sit there with my stomach churning.

I hate that she was caught in our storm. She deserves better than that.

I look over at Emryn, and she's also sitting there—staring at her plate and not eating. I know she is thinking the same thing I am. We can't change it now, though. We have to move forward and make sure Avery isn't pulled down in our problems again.

I reach over the table and squeeze Emryn's hand like I did with Avery's moments ago. We are in this together now. We both have regrets, but we can't wallow in them.

She looks up from her plate, tears brimming her eyes.

"I love you," I mouth.

She nods her head but doesn't say it back. The unease in my stomach churns a little more. I won't push her to say it, just like I didn't last night, but it still stings a little that she hasn't.

Chapter 22

Emryn

When Brooks pulls the truck into the church's parking lot, my parent's vehicle is already there. I can't decide if that makes this less daunting or more.

Butterflies dance in my stomach. I don't know why I'm so nervous. This is the church I attended as a little girl. It's the one that Brooks and I got married in, but it's been a while since I've been here.

Brooks opens my door, and I fidget with my skirt as he unbuckles Avery out of her car seat.

"Deep breaths, Em," Brooks says, grabbing my hand and scooping Avery up in the other arm.

Hand in hand, we walk to the steps of the church.

There's a moment when we reach the bottom of the stairs that Brooks hesitates. His steps falter—a mask shutters over his features—but then he looks between me and our daughter, squares his shoulders, and moves forward. My heart aches for him.

His memories here are hard—losing his mom was hard.

I squeeze his hand, hoping he takes some of the same comfort he offered me. He squeezes back and gives me a small smile before pulling the door open for us to step through.

When we step inside, it's alive with voices as people make their way to their seats. Avery catches a glimpse of Mom, Dad, and Tayte at the front and takes off towards them.

I look over my shoulder to make sure that Brooks is following but find him standing still, staring at the back pew. My eyes follow his line of sight and stop when they reach the spot he is staring at.

Kip Montgomery sits in the very last pew, dressed in a new button-up, with his hair combed back neatly.

The butterflies that were in my stomach when we walked in turn into raging monsters.

A man steps in front of Brooks and shakes his hand, dragging his attention away from Kip, but Brooks keeps glancing over every few seconds. When the man finally moves to take his seat, Brooks steps towards Kip. I follow behind him, worried about what this confrontation might turn into.

Whenever Kip and Brooks are in the same room together, they can't help but be at each other's throats.

I can't blame Brooks. There are a lot of hard feelings there, but I would guess those feelings are exacerbated here in the place where Brooks felt most abandoned by the man.

Hurt and anger war on his face as he approaches his dad, and my heart breaks for him.

"Brooks," Kip starts, "before you say anything, I'm not here to cause trouble. If you want me to leave, just say the word."

I place my hand on Brooks's shoulder so he knows I'm here.

He doesn't have to face this alone—I hope he knows that.

But when he shakes my hand off his shoulder, I worry that he doesn't.

"You know what, Kip," Brooks says, looking around at the church, "this is not my house, and from what I'm told, all are welcome here, but that doesn't mean I'm ready to sit beside you and pretend we are one big happy family—not here at least. But—we are having a cookout at our house next weekend. Why don't you join us?"

I hold my breath while we wait for Kip's answer. I don't know what made Brooks offer, but I'll support him through this new phase in their relationship.

Kip gives a jerky nod.

My cheeks puff out as I let out my breath, and Brooks places his hand on my back, leading us to the front pew where my parents are sitting with Avery.

As we walk, I lean closer to Brooks and whisper, "I'm proud of you."

The dimple pokes in on his cheek, but he doesn't say anything back.

We settle in as the announcements are made, but now and again, I catch Brooks glancing back over his shoulder.

By the time Pastor Evert takes the pulpit, Brooks has glanced back at his dad ten times.

My dad leans over and whispers something to Brooks, and I see my husband's lips lift at the corners. I don't need to know what Dad said to him. It's enough for me to know that Brooks can rely on my dad—even if he doesn't realize it.

"Good morning, everyone," Pastor Evert begins. "Today, we'll be in the book of Philippians, so if you could open your Bibles, we'll begin."

There's a rustling of paper as people flip through pages in Bibles that have seen their fair share of wear.

"In the book of Philippians, Paul is in jail. He's writing to the Phillipian church. His circumstances look dire to many who look at them. But God." Pastor Evert stops and looks around, taking his time as he makes eye contact with each person in the congregation. "Many of you may say, now Pastor, 'But God' isn't a full sentence, but I say it's the only sentence you need."

He wipes the sweat from his brow and grabs a glass of water from the pulpit.

"Let me put it this way. You're financially strapped. But God—. You can't find a job. But God—. You are going through a divorce. But God—."

My stomach churns at his last words. They hit a little too close to home—to a place where Brooks and I almost were. I didn't want to admit how close we were to a divorce, even after I left, but if we hadn't gone to that first therapy session, I don't know if we would be sitting in this church together today.

"All these are situations where we worry. We are human. Worry comes naturally to us, but Paul tells the church that we don't have to worry with God. He instructs us to pray, and God will give us the peace we seek."

Looking down, I fiddle with the corner of my Bible. Pastor Evert is feeding my soul.

I love Brooks, but I'm terrified of losing myself in our marriage again when I'm just starting to find where I fit.

I didn't realize I had that fear until Brooks told me he loved me, and then I let it be a wedge that slipped between me and my husband. Each time Brooks said it, I wanted to tell him how much I loved him too, but I was afraid that if I did, I would start to lose the woman I've worked hard to find.

Listening to Pastor Evert, I realize I can't keep worrying about it. I have to trust that God knows what he is doing in my marriage—and life—and that my husband loves me enough to help me grow. I'm not the same woman I was a few months ago. I've changed—found me outside of Brooks—it's made our marriage stronger because of it.

Avery squirms in her seat as the sermon comes to a close. She's not used to sitting this long, but she did well for her age—only trying to climb under the pews one or two times.

At Pastor Evert's dismissal, we all rise to leave, and Mom waves her hand from the other side of the pew to signal for me to wait. I stop in the aisle, right outside the pew, until she slips out.

Once she's standing beside me, she says, "We're having Sunday dinner at our house. Why don't you all come? Your brother will be there. Plus, Pastor Evert and his wife are coming as well."

I look at Brooks, but he's standing halfway up the aisle, staring back at where his dad sat during the sermon. It's empty now. Kip must have slipped out during the altar call.

There's a deep crease between Brooks's eyebrows.

He's starting to heal from the things that have haunted him his whole life, but I don't imagine it's easy.

"Let me go ask Brooks," I say.

I walk down the aisle, stopping short of him, and place my hand on his shoulder. He turns his head towards me, and gone is the pain that marred his face moments ago.

"Mom said they're having Sunday dinner at their house. Do you want to go?" I ask.

His fingers find a strand of my hair, tugging on it gently.

"I think that would be nice," he replies.

I meet his smile with one of my own and turn back to tell my mom we will meet them at the house.

She nods, and we gather Avery to head to the car.

As we walk to the car, he laces his fingers with mine, and peace fills my soul. This is how it should have been all along.

When we get to the truck, he drops my hand to open my door. In that one action, I feel cherished. I never wanted big things from Brooks— just the little things.

I slip into the car, and he closes the door behind me. Taking Avery by the hand, he opens her door and lifts her into her car seat. Avery looks up at him and smiles, and in that moment, I know that her definition of love will always be based on how her daddy loves her. Every guy in her life will have to live up to the standard her dad set.

Brooks finishes buckling her in before he walks around and climbs into his seat.

"How did you feel about being back here today?" he asks, starting the car and pulling out on the highway.

"I felt quiet."

His eyes flick to me—questioning—before returning to the road. "What do you mean quiet?"

"I don't know. It's hard to explain. For the last year, there have been these constant voices of worry in my head about us—and me—but when I walked into that church with you today, those voices just kind of stopped. I know that probably won't last because I tend to worry about everything, but it's nice to have a place where I know I can find the quiet—even for a moment."

Brooks takes my hand and presses his lips against my knuckles.

"I'm glad you found that. I know we've struggled this last year. I wasn't there for you as you needed me to be, but I want to be now. And yeah—maybe I'll mess up sometimes, but I need you to know I'm trying, okay?"

I nod and swallow hard against the emotion in my throat. "I love you, Brooks."

The words drop like a weight between us. I realized in church I've been holding back from telling him that because I was afraid, but he deserves to know that he is loved and that I'm here to stay too.

I glance over and see love swimming in his eyes. I squeeze his fingers so he knows I'm right there with him.

"I love you too, pretty girl," he says.

"You know," I start, "If you had asked me two months ago if we would be sitting here working on ourselves and our marriage, I would have called you a liar. I thought we were destined for divorce, but I've seen the change in you. I've changed too. I'm proud of both of us."

"I'm proud of us too," he says, squeezing my hand.

"Me too," Avery yells from the backseat.

I toss my head back and laugh. It's freeing.

161

Chapter 23

Emryn

"They're here," Avery yells from the front window. She's been waiting there since she got up this morning, only moving when I made her take a bath and eat.

When I walk into the living room, she's bouncing up and down on her toes, ready to burst with the energy trapped inside her.

"Can I open the door now?" she asks. "Can I?"

"Sure, but don't tackle anybody before they make it inside."

Avery takes off at top speed, and I follow behind.

Brooks chuckles from the stairs when she zooms past him, nearly tripping over the rug in her haste. I catch his eye and shake my head, and his laugh booms deeper than before—sending tingles along my arms.

I could listen to him laugh for the rest of my life.

He takes the rest of the steps two at a time, landing at the bottom at the same time Avery slings open the door.

"Uncle Tater-tot," Avery squeals, jumping into his arms. Tayte's brows furrow, and I pull my shirt over my nose, hiding my snicker. He shoots me a glare over the top of Avery's head as I shrug one shoulder. I can't help that she's in the stage where she repeats everything I say. The name caught on during a day when he was being especially annoying. She heard, and it stuck. Now, he will be forever deemed "Uncle Tater-tot."

Brooks leans in behind me, his hard chest pressing against my back, and suddenly, that's all I can think about. The man never works out, but man does physical labor do something for him.

"I think you did that on purpose," he says. His breath fans against my ear as he tilts his head beside mine, his lips brushing against me as he speaks.

"I don't know what you're talking about," I say, leaning further into him.

"Mmm-hmm." The sound rumbles in his chest, vibrating against my back.

Tayte looks over at us and sticks his finger in his mouth, gagging, and Avery scrunches up her nose, repeating the motion.

Laughter erupts around me—first Tayte, then Brooks.

I slap each of them on the head respectively and then point out the open front door.

"Look," I say. "Mom and Dad just pulled in. I told her to bring one dish, but you know Mom, she can't attend a function without bringing a four-course meal. You two get out there and help her before you corrupt my daughter further."

Tayte salutes me, and then army marches out the door and down the steps with Avery in his arms, giggling at his antics. My brother is a great uncle. He would be a good dad if he ever decided to settle down, but no one has ever held his attention for long.

I roll my eyes and follow him off the porch with Brooks close behind me.

At the car, Mom is already unloading several glass dishes. The woman doesn't know the meaning of too much food.

"Mom, I told you that I had it taken care of. You didn't have to bring this much."

She narrows her eyes at me and says, "Emryn Grace, a good guest never comes empty-handed."

Throwing my hands up in surrender, I mumble, "I didn't realize that meant bringing the whole house."

"I heard that," she calls over her shoulder as she unloads food containers and shoves them into my dad's hands.

Placing Avery down on the ground, Tayte loads his arms too. More cars pile into the driveway as Brooks takes the rest of the dishes from my mom.

In total, she brought three side dishes, two kinds of meat, and a dessert.

We will be eating for days.

As the men take the food inside, I step aside and allow the other cars to pull into the driveway alongside the front porch.

Pastor Evert and his wife are the first out of their car. Mrs. Evert's hair is red today. The last time it was red, well—the town, as a whole, does not talk about the last time.

"Hi, Emmie girl," Mrs. Evert says, carrying a cobbler dish in front of her.

"Hello, ma'am. How are you?" I ask.

The usually sweet, erratic elderly woman sends a hateful glare at her husband standing beside her. She shoves her hands on her hips and looks back at me. "We all have our days, Emryn. We all have our days."

Her husband must have the patience of Job because he merely gives a shake of his head and leads her away towards the house.

The red hair makes sense now.

I hate that the two are fighting, but, in a way, it's nice to see the reality of marriage. It's not always the honeymoon stage, but it doesn't have to stay a struggle either.

Tayte steps back onto the porch, having delivered the food to the kitchen, and Avery skips behind him—imitating his every move.

I shudder at the thought of what that means for me later.

164

Turning to the other car that pulled in, I see Mia and her boyfriend, Chase, standing by her car. I've never met the guy, but I have mixed feelings about him. Mia seems to love him, but she also flinches whenever he's brought up in our conversations. The movement is almost imperceptible, but it's there all the same. I'm glad she brought him today because I've wanted to scope him out. She is the kindest soul I've ever met. She doesn't deserve to be with a jerk. I hope I'm wrong about him, but I don't think I am from the look of them now.

At the front of the car, Mia is juggling several dishes in her hands as Chase stands back and watches. I step forward to help her, but Tayte must notice at the same time as I do. He jumps over the railing of the raised porch and lands with a thud next to the couple.

Tayte's eyes are menacing—a look I've never seen on my usually laid-back big brother. Anger flashes across his features as he takes the food from Mia's hand.

"Here, let me show you how to help a lady," he says, glaring at Chase and shoving the plates into his hands.

Chase grunts as the plates slip through his fingers and shove into his stomach with enough force to cause him to step back.

"Hey, man. What's your problem?" he asks, stepping up until he's toe to toe with my brother.

Chase is tall, but my brother is taller. The two men glare at each other—a stark contrast to the other. Tayte's blond hair is a halo compared to the darkness of the other man.

Mia steps between the two, looking more irritated than I have ever seen her.

Man, what is with people today?

"What are you doing here?" she asks Tayte.

"You two know each other?" Chase asks from behind Mia.

They ignore him, and he lets out a huff of irritation.

Tayte's lips flatten as he looks from Mia to her boyfriend behind her.

"It looks like I'm saving you—again," he answers.

I wasn't aware that they knew each other, which is saying a lot since one of them is my brother. That little jerk has been hiding things from me.

My eyes ping-pong back and forth between the pair. Tayte's hands are clenched into fists, but his upper body is leaning toward Mia as if he wants to protect her and throttle her simultaneously.

Interesting.

"I was fine. If I needed help, I would have asked Chase, and he would have helped me without your interference," Mia scoffs.

"Yeah, it looked like it—just like he was there the last time, right?" Tayte's tone is flat when he answers.

"Last time? What is he talking about, Mia?" Chase bristles.

I step up before a fight can ensue. Tayte's not a guy who gets irritated easily, but it's rolling off him in waves right now.

"Mia, I didn't realize you knew my brother. Small world," I say, jabbing my elbow into Tayte's stomach so he stops glaring at Chase.

I don't know this side of my brother. It's strange.

"Um—actually, do you remember how I told you I was moving last weekend and didn't need your help because Chase would be there? It turns out your brother is my neighbor. I didn't know he was your brother, though. Did aliens raise him or something?" Mia asks.

I grin. There's the Mia I know. Tayte doesn't find the humor in her remark and instead merely grunts as he walks away.

"Don't worry, Emryn," Mia says loud enough for Tayte to hear as he walks away. "I won't judge you because your brother has no manners."

I bite my lip to keep from belly laughing. She grabs the containers back from Chase, who doesn't put up a fight to carry them for her, and as we are heading up the porch steps, I look back at my brother. He's pushing Avery on the swing in the front yard. His shoulders are tense as if he knows he's being watched, but he doesn't turn around.

166

———————————————

I take Mia on a tour of the house, and we leave Chase in the living room, talking to my parents. Well—my parents are talking. He is just standing there, studiously ignoring them and scrolling through his phone.

"Spill," I say once we are upstairs in Brooks's office.

She looks around, thumbing through the bookshelf like it's the most exciting thing in the world.

"About what?" she asks as if she wasn't there for that whole scene downstairs.

"Mia."

"Fine," she says, flopping down on the office chair. "The day I moved in, I told you I didn't need your help because Chase would be there. He—um—forgot, so I was moving things in on my own. Your brother saw and came over and helped. The end."

"From what I witnessed downstairs, that does not seem like the end."

"Okay, maybe it's not the end. Maybe I was frustrated with Chase, and when your brother came over to help, I told him that the entire male population wasn't worth a penny. And maybe I said more than that, but I can't quite remember."

She looks down at her feet, pink staining her cheeks.

"So—" I say carefully. "How did Tayte react to your—tangent?"

At this point, Mia's cheeks are the color of an apple. "That's the thing. He ignored my whole breakdown, took the box I was carrying from me, and then proceeded to spend the rest of the afternoon helping me unload the rest of my stuff despite the hundreds of times I protested."

I feign shock, opening my mouth and placing my hand over it. "What a monster my brother is."

Mia rolls her eyes and says, "Not a monster, but bossy—very, very bossy."

"Welcome to the club. He's been bossing me around since I was

167

born," I hesitate a moment before I ask the question I've been holding back. "What about Chase? Are things okay there?"

She doesn't meet my eye, thumbing through a book she's picked off the bookshelf.

"Yeah, everything is great. He's just—not a social person—and he forgets things, but I love him. What about you and Brooks? How are things since you've moved back in?"

I don't believe her, but I can see how tears swim in her eyes. There was a time when I wasn't ready to face my failing relationship either, but when the time comes, and she's ready to open her eyes to what's happening, I'll be there for her.

"I'm happy, Mia. This feels like it did when we first got married—but, at the same time, that scares me."

Her brows dip, "Scares you how?"

I shrug, sitting on the edge of the desk. "I never saw us ending up in a place where we were more roommates than husband and wife. What if we end up there again? What if this is just the honeymoon phase?"

Mia's eyes soften. "I don't think that will happen again. You both know what it takes now. You've been in that place and reflected on how you got there. It's up to both of you to be intentional about your decisions. That's the way you avoid it."

Chapter 24

Brooks

"Have you tried calling your dad?" Emryn asks from behind me.

The party is in full swing inside, but I'm standing on the front porch, leaning against one of the posts—lost in my thoughts. The party is nice, but I needed a minute. One minute, and then I'll wipe away the disappointment and return to the people who have never let me down. That's all I've ever allowed myself when it comes to Kip—one minute.

I don't turn around to look at Emryn but stand looking out—watching as the sun dips over the horizon.

"He's an hour late—probably not coming," I say, then shrug. "I didn't expect him to."

Emryn's arms slip around my waist, her front pressing against my back. Her arms squeeze me tight enough to hold together my broken pieces.

"Maybe you didn't expect him to, but I think you hoped. He could be just running late."

I love her innocence—the feeling of never knowing what it means to be let down by her parents—but I've been let down by Kip more times than I can count. I prepared myself for this when I invited him. You don't survive an alcoholic father unless you wrap yourself in armor.

169

For me, that armor came by way of expecting little from him—even when others expect the best.

Turning in her arms, I drop a kiss on the crown of her hair.

"He's not coming, Emryn, but it's fine. *I'm* fine."

Her eyes are sad for me, and that's the part I hate the most—the pity. I brush my knuckles along her cheek as her arms hold me tighter. "Don't feel sorry for me, darling. I have everyone I need right here."

Her smile is sad as we stand there, holding one another.

As crickets and frogs sing around us, gravel crunches from the driveway. Emryn lifts onto her toes to look over my shoulder, and a broad smile spreads across her lips. A dimple pokes in on her cheek, and I'm mesmerized by that one movement.

"Maybe it's time for you to learn that people won't always let you down," she says, patting my chest and walking back inside.

My eyes never leave her, taking her in through the screen door until she disappears into the kitchen.

Even after she's gone, it takes a moment before I can turn around because I know who's there, and I don't know how to feel about the fact that he showed.

I turn around, and Kip is stepping out of his truck. He's holding a clear plastic container full of potato salad, the bar code sticker still stuck to the side, and on top of it, there's a bouquet of gas station flowers. Staying on the porch, I let him come to me.

He reaches the bottom of the stairs and stops. Looking up at me, he fidgets with the sticker on the potato salad.

"You're here," I say—stupid because obviously he's here, but I've never just carried on small talk with the man.

"I'm sorry I'm late," he says, rubbing the back of his neck. "I didn't want to come empty handed, but there's a reason your mom always cooked. I burnt the dish I was going to bring. I had to stop by the store to grab something else. These are for Emryn."

He shoves the flowers up at me, and I take them from his hands.

"She'll love them. Thanks."

"Sure," he says, shuffling his feet.

I wish Emryn hadn't gone back inside.

"Do you—uh—want to come in?" I ask, pointing over my shoulder at the door.

He shakes his head. "I was hoping we could talk a minute."

His eyes flit from me and back to the ground as if he expects me to say no. That would have been true a few weeks ago, but I promised myself I would try for the sake of my family.

Tilting my head towards the rocking chairs, I ask, "Want to sit a minute?"

He nods, and I step back to let him climb the steps.

Our boots knock against the wooden porch as we walk over the edge where the rocking chairs are sitting. Kip takes a seat, the potato salad in his lap like a shield against me. The flowers sit in mine the same way.

"Did you call about that job?" he asks.

My hackles rise.

"No," I grit out.

He swallows hard and nods.

"I think it would be a good opportunity for you—for us."

I squint at him, studying how he rocks back and forth without looking at me. Of course, there's something in it for him—there always is.

"Us?" I ask, feeling him out to see if he will be honest for once. "Are you making a commission or something?"

He was secretive when I asked him where the job opportunity came from. Was that because he was gaining something from it?

"No, I just—I've made a lot of mistakes in my lifetime, Brooks, and I'm trying to fix them."

171

I don't think that's the full answer, but he came here to try tonight, and I can at least give him the benefit of the doubt.

Besides, people's true colors always come out eventually.

Chapter 25

Emryn

I toss the curling iron down on the bathroom counter. Toss is too generous of a word. With the way it bounced off the counter onto the floor, it's more like I threw it down.

The one day I need my hair to cooperate, it doesn't. Instead, I look like I've stuck my finger in an electrical socket.

I let out a frustrated scream, trying to expel my nerves.

Tayte set up a meeting with the dean at Hanlin University like he said he would, and I'm meeting him today at his office.

If I can get there. Everything has gone wrong—and I do mean everything.

My alarm didn't go off. I've changed my clothes a hundred times because nothing fits right. I feel frumpy, and I'm missing one shoe.

ONE. SHOE.

The bed calls my name, begging me to restart this day, but I can't.

I bend over to pick up the curling iron, and at the same time, the bathroom door swings open. Startled, I jump, cracking my elbow on the corner of the sink.

"Stinking sink," I yell, kicking at it several times to release some frustration.

Brooks stands in the doorway, puffing air and looking around frantically as I throw my tissy fit.

I can admit it's not a good look.

"What is it? What's wrong?" he asks between puffs. His chest heaves up and down as he assesses me for injuries. Aside from my elbow, he finds none.

"Did you just run up here?" I ask, letting my tantrum subside.

He narrows his eyes.

"I heard screaming. Of course, I ran. You sounded like you were having a toe cut off."

Some of the tension that's filled my shoulders all morning starts to loosen as a laugh bubbles out. It's loud and bordering on hysterical—maybe even tears—but I can't control it.

Brooks watches me, bewildered by what's happening.

As I continue laughing, he steps forward like he's approaching a wild animal that is seconds away from biting him. Who knows, at this point, I just might.

When he gets close enough, he places his palms on each side of my cheeks and twists my head from side to side, examining me.

"Are you okay? Did you hit your head or something?"

My laughter notches up, and tears stream from my eyes. I can't catch my breath.

An uncomfortable laugh leaves Brooks's lips, and a look of concern flits through his eyes.

I try again to catch my breath, but the air won't reach the bottom of my lungs. Uncontrollable laughter turns into uncontrollable tears as panic takes over.

Brooks's hands leave my face and reach for my waist. His fingers dig into my hips as he picks me up and places me on the sink.

"Hey, look at me, pretty girl," he says.

I lift my chin and look at him, but his face is a blur. His shoulder is the perfect height for me to lay my head on. One of his hands stays on my hip, and the other rubs circles on my back.

My sobs slow to hiccups, but Brooks doesn't stop touching me. I might splinter into a million tiny pieces if he does.

"Tell me what this is all about," he whispers against the shell of my ear.

"You'll think it's silly," I say.

His fingers tangle in my hair at the base of my neck, and he gently pulls my head back so I'm staring at him, "I will never think anything important to you is silly."

I chew on my bottom lip, trying to figure out how to explain it to him.

"It's just—" I say. "Sometimes, there are days when everything keeps going wrong, and I have a hundred things I need to get done. Plus, I've felt guilty for subbing the last couple of weeks because I'm taking time away from Avery. That's where I should devote my time. I'm a mom and a wife. How can I be a student too? I'm a *mess*."

His thumb rubs along my neck.

"Emryn, first of all, we are all messy sometimes. Do you think I'm not messy—that I don't have things that bother me or ruin my day? I do. But—let's address that guilt. You are allowed to be more than a mom and wife. Your identity is not rooted in those two things."

What I'm not telling him is that I'm scared that my relationship with my daughter will suffer if I do something for myself.

Will Avery grow up feeling like I didn't give her enough of myself? Will she think that I put other things above her?

"Talk to me, Emryn. Show me your heart."

I can't meet his eyes. I look everywhere but at him. The ceiling. The door. The top of his forehead.

"What if Avery thinks I don't love her? What if I can't be a good mom, wife, and student?"

Dropping my head against his collarbone, I let out a huff. Tears slip from the corner of my eyes and drip off the end of my nose, soaking into the soft cotton of his t-shirt. His hands run down the length of my hair.

"She will always know that you love her—your love can't be diluted. As for doing it all—mom, wife, student—you don't have to do it alone. I know in the past, I was blind to all the things that you do, but I see it now. I'm here."

And that's all I can ask for.

————————————

The first thing I notice about Hanlin University campus is the trees. They are everywhere—lining the sidewalks, framing the buildings. They are aflame with color, popping out against the brick.

Fall is here.

I watch as the wind picks up a leaf from a branch and floats it to the ground.

This is my favorite time of year—the crisp smell of the air and the chill that's just enough for a cozy jacket—all of it.

There's beauty in change, and I'm reminded of that every time fall comes around. It's a reminder that I desperately needed today. Change is good, but it doesn't make it any less difficult. I'm used to being *passive*, letting change pass me by.

The last few months have been about growth for me, and today is another big step toward finding this new version of myself.

The second thing I notice is how young everyone looks as they rush to class with their backpacks slung over one shoulder. I'm twenty-eight, and I've never felt old until this moment.

I glance at my watch, checking the time before I head toward the building to my left.

When I reach the top of the steps, I take one big breath in and let the chill in the air burn in my lungs before releasing it and opening the door to the education building.

My meeting is on the third floor, but I'm too anxious to climb into an elevator with other people. I need to burn out some of this energy before I take it into the meeting with me, so I opt for the stairs.

By the time I reach the third floor, I'm puffing air and convinced that I should add working out to my new transformation.

I check the office number on my phone and veer to the right of the hallway, walking until I reach the door labeled 401.

Shaking the nerves from my hands, I flex my fingers and reach up to knock on the door.

"Come in," a deep voice booms from the other side.

I hesitate one more minute before opening the door and stepping into the office.

The interior is modern, with sleek lines and furniture. In the center of the room is a large desk. An older man sits behind it, his dark skin a contrast to his white beard.

He stands when I step further into the room, and I stretch out my hand towards him. He takes it, his grip strong.

"Good afternoon, sir. I'm Emryn Montgomery."

"No need for formalities. You can call me Jack," he says, motioning for me to sit.

"Okay, Jack. I appreciate you meeting me today."

"It was my pleasure, young lady. Your brother was quite the character when we met. He left an impression."

A nervous chuckle slips out as I fiddle with the bottom of my shirt. "I can only imagine."

"Let's talk about you, shall we?" Jack asks.

I grip the hem of my shirt tighter, unsure what he wants to know. There isn't much to say about myself other than I've been a mom and a wife for the better part of my life.

"Um—what is it you would like to know?"

"We can start with something easy. Why is it you've decided to come back to school?"

The answer is easy, but I worry about what he will think about it. My eyes roam to my lap, staying there as I say, "When I was in college, my husband, Brooks, proposed. At the time, we were long-distance. I was young and in love and didn't realize I needed an identity outside of him. As I've gotten older, I've realized that while I love my husband, I need to find a place where I fit—where I feel like the woman I am isn't lost in everyone else."

There's a moment before Jack responds, and I look up to find him studying me.

"You say all of this like you're ashamed. Which part is it that makes you hesitant to tell your story?"

I squirm in my seat—feeling like he can see through to the heart of me.

"I'm not ashamed—not really. I think embarrassed would be a better word. I'm twenty-eight years old. I'm a mom and a wife. I'm going to sit in a class with eighteen year old kids. Maybe I missed my shot."

"Emryn, I can help you put that fear at rest. Before I was a dean, I was a professor in this school for many years. Do you know how many people in my classroom were in the same position you are?"

Shaking my head, my hair falls around my shoulders.

"Many. Don't be afraid to find who you are. Our lives are meant for growth. What fun would it be if we stayed the same person our whole life?"

I find myself smiling at the man who doesn't know me but is willing to offer me comfort anyway. I'm afraid of stepping out of my comfort zone—of failing Avery as I do—but I have people surrounding me who are willing to help me push past that fear.

Chapter 26

Brooks

I'm sitting at the table in the kitchen with bills piled up all around me. The door to the garage opens, and Emryn walks in. She's radiant—her lips curving up just enough to hint at her dimple. My heart stutters as I take her in. I'm glad to see the smile back on her face. I hated seeing her broken like she was this morning.

"I take it the meeting went well," I say, sweeping the papers into a pile and stuffing them under my laptop. I don't want to ruin her mood right now with bills. We can talk about them later—this moment is about her.

I scoot my chair out and pull her down into my lap. She lets out a squeal before wrapping her arms around my neck and twirling my hair between her fingers.

"I loved it there," she says. "The campus was beautiful, and I learned a lot from Jack."

"Jack?" I question.

She nods, "He's the dean I met with today. Thanks to him—and you—I feel a little more settled about things now."

"That's great, Emryn. I'm proud of you."

I love that today went well for her. The papers peek out from under my computer, catching my attention. She deserves to find a place she fits, but I can't help thinking about where my life is going now. My mind goes back to the one letter she wrote. She said she was finding herself and hoped that when she did, we would be moving in the same direction.

I'm not sure that's what we are doing. She's moving forward—finding who she is—while I'm motionless, unable to move past the mistakes that have led me here.

I can't find a job, and bills are coming in faster than I expected. I know that Jonathan's offer is still on the table, but something holds me back whenever I pick up the phone and tell him I'll take it.

Then there's the card that my dad gave me.

I haven't taken it from my wallet since he gave it to me, but it hasn't left my mind.

My whole life, I've promised that I would be the one to take care of my family—that I wouldn't have to rely on someone else. If I take the job with Emryn's dad, I'll only get it because I married his daughter.

On the other hand, the interview with Grayson Lewis came from my dad. That alone is a red flag, especially knowing he will benefit from it. It's not that I don't want him to benefit, but he hasn't been honest about it. At the same time, the position comes with an interview. That means that, in a way, the job would come on my own merit.

"Thank you for supporting me," Emryn says, pulling me out of my downward spiral as she rubs one hand across the scruff of my jaw.

I close my eyes and press my jaw tighter to her hand.

"Emryn, you never have to thank me for supporting you. I'll be your cheerleader whenever you need me to be."

"I'll get you a pair of pompoms for Christmas then," she giggles, and heat warms my chest.

She's messing with me, but she doesn't realize that I would wave those pompoms around with pride if it meant that I was supporting her.

"Bring them on, pretty girl," I say, placing a kiss on her temple.

Her smile is infectious.

"How was Avery today?" she asks.

"Wild as always. She wanted to explore the woods today, so we went for a walk. Then, when we got back, I made lunch. She's sleeping now. I think I wore her out."

I stretch and let out a big yawn. Emryn looks me over, studying me closely.

"Looks like she isn't the only one that's worn out. Can't keep up, old man?"

I narrow my eyes at her.

"Who are you calling old man?"

She pushes out of my lap, kisses my cheek, and takes off running.

"You," she calls over her shoulder.

"We're the same age," I yell, chasing after her.

———————————

Later that evening, Emryn is out for ice cream with Avery, her way of making up for the time she spent away from Avery today, and I'm sitting back at the kitchen table, scrolling through job listings.

My guilt sits like a mountain on my shoulders. When I filed for bankruptcy, I knew I could provide for us for six months, but the days and our finances are dwindling while the bills keep coming in. I never dreamed it would take this long to find a new position.

I drop my head into my hands, pushing my hat up and rubbing the heels of my palm against the headache forming in my forehead.

The mountain of guilt on my shoulder is pulling me down, telling me that if I don't get this figured out soon, I could lose my family again—which isn't an option I want to consider.

Having Emryn and Avery walk out the door was too much for me the first time. I won't be able to handle it a second time.

Pushing away from the table, I stand, knocking the chair over.

I need to figure something out soon. I don't have time to waste any longer.

One thing is for sure—I can't bring myself to rely on Jonathan. The man has already done enough for me that I'll never be able to repay him for. I can't ask more of him.

Pulling my wallet out of my pocket, I slip the card into my fingers. It's a flimsy piece of card stock, but it might as well weigh a thousand pounds—or maybe it's just the weight of what I'm about to do.

For the first time in my life, I'm about to put faith in my dad, and that's scary.

Grabbing my phone from the table, I flick my thumb over the screen, unlocking it. My fingers hover over each number before I punch them in. I'm slow—methodical—giving myself time to back out, but when I catch a glimpse of the papers sticking out from beneath my computer, I know I won't.

I count the rings.

Ring.

One.

Ring.

Two.

Ring.

Three.

Then, "Grayson Lewis." A gruff voice answers on the other side.

For a moment, I don't say anything. I pull the phone away from my ear and check the number against the one on the card. I didn't think this would be Grayson's direct line. I figured I would get an assistant and set up the interview with them.

I try to connect the puzzle pieces between the card, my dad, and Grayson, but I can't get a clear picture. I'm not sure how my dad got a direct line to the CEO of one of the biggest companies in the area. There's a story here, and for some reason, my gut warns me from continuing this call. Grayson is not the type of guy my dad usually knows.

I don't have time to debate my next step. On the other end, Grayson's voice rumbles. "Hello?"

"Oh yes, sorry," I say, clearing my throat. "My name is Brooks Montgomery. I'm calling in regards to an interview."

There's a beat of silence where I'm left questioning if my dad set me up to look like a fool, but then Grayson answers, "Let me check my calendar."

I wait while I hear the rustling of papers.

"Let's do the twenty-seventh at four o'clock." He says in a voice that leaves no question whether the date and time are open for discussion.

My stomach drops, sending up flares about this interview.

That's the day of Emryn's parent's anniversary party.

I won't get another chance if I don't take the interview now. Once again, my eyes travel to the bills on the table.

"I'll be there," I say.

"I'll send you a text with the information," Grayson says, hanging up without a goodbye.

I pull the phone from my ear and stare at it.

I'm beginning to think the rumors about Grayson being hard to work for are true.

Placing the phone down on the counter, I start pacing the kitchen.

There's an hour between when the interview starts and when I have to be at the party. I could make it. Plus, Emryn is going early to set up. I don't have to tell her about the interview until I know I have the job—it can be a surprise.

That only leaves one more thing for me to take care of. I am supposed to have Avery with me while Emryn sets up, but she can't go with me to the interview.

I tap my finger against my chin, trying to come up with a solution— only one person comes to mind.

Chapter 27

Emryn

I slip the satin dress over my head, careful not to tear down my up-do. It pools around my feet as it slides to the floor. Once it's on, I turn to look in the mirror, and tears brim my eyes when I catch a glimpse of the woman looking back at me. The dress is long and black with a slit that comes to mid-thigh. At the top, one strap slashes dramatically across my shoulder, but it's not the dress I'm looking at.

There's a contentment on my face that I haven't seen in a long time. The tinge of red along my cheeks and the way my lips tip up in a smile are reminders of the happiness I've felt over the last few weeks. This woman looking back at me is the person I've been searching for.

The door behind me creaks open, and Brooks steps into the room dressed in his suit.

The man is so handsome it should be illegal. He cleaned up his beard but still left it long enough that I could slide my hand along his jaw and feel the prickle against my skin. A shiver runs up my spine at the thought. His broad shoulders fill out his suit in a way that screams masculinity. It's his eyes that hold my attention, though. The blue is as clear as ice, but there's a heat there that threatens to melt me with just one scorching look.

He stares at me, slipping his gaze down to my black stilettos and gliding his eyes *up, up, up* until he meets mine—and then he continues to stare.

I clear my throat, waiting for him to say something, and when he doesn't, I speak first.

"You look nice," I say. Still, he continues to stare.

"Earth to, Brooks," I say, waving my hand to wake him from his trance. "Is the dress too much?"

Suddenly, I'm self-conscious, crossing my arms over my stomach to hide some of the mom pooch I know sticks out. In a flash, he breaks out of his daze and moves across the room like a predator on the hunt.

My breath catches in my throat, and I take an involuntary step back. He follows until there's no more room for me to retreat—my shoulders pressed against the wall behind me.

Brooks reaches out, sliding his hand across my hip.

The heat of his hand scorches through the cold satin, and prickles of awareness run over my skin. There's fire in his eyes as he clears his throat to speak. "Since I was six and thought girls had cooties, you have always had my attention. You were beautiful the day I married you on the playground, and you have only become more beautiful with age. You could be wearing a potato sack, and I would still think that you are the prettiest girl in the room."

His voice is gruff, but I can hear the truth in his words.

I lean in and place my lips gently against his, careful not to smudge all my lipstick off, but one small taste isn't enough. Brooks's hand moves from my hip to frame my face as he pulls me back in—kissing me until my lipstick is smeared against his lips.

Pulling back, I rub my thumb across the bottom of his lip and wipe away all traces of where my lips covered his.

There's no hiding the heat in his eyes. They are a mirror reflecting the truth of his word. In his eyes, I'm strong and beautiful.

He dips his head so his forehead falls against mine.

"Thank you for seeing me again." Our lips brush as I say the words, but he's not content with near kisses tonight. He deepens it, pushing his fingers into my hair, and I'm powerless to resist—not that I would want to.

When my lipstick is gone, and strands are falling from my hair, he takes a step back, releasing me.

Strands of hair fall around my face, and I turn back to the mirror to check the damage. The curls are still there, but the up-do isn't salvageable.

"You ruined my hair," I say, throwing him an exasperated glare through the mirror—though it's only half exasperated. I'll let him ruin my hair any day if it means he kisses me like that. I've spent too long missing them.

When I look at him, he's wearing a smirk that does funny things to my heart.

"I can't say I'm sorry," he chuckles darkly.

I spin around and place my hands on his chest, pushing him towards the door.

"You're being banished. You're too distracting, and now I have to fix my hair again, so shoo."

I give him one last shove through the door, but he grabs a hold of my wrist and pulls me towards him. I crash into his chest as he reaches up and pulls the remaining clips from my hair.

He leans down so his cheek is pressed against mine. I can feel his stubble scratching against my skin, "Leave it down. It's my favorite look on you."

Then he's stepping back, winking, and leaving me smiling after him.

———————————

After rearranging the curls to frame my face and reapplying lipstick, I gather the rest of my stuff, kiss Avery goodbye, and wave to Brooks.

He pokes out his lips and pouts because I don't kiss him too, but I've been there and done that today—it left me with a racing heart and running late.

Instead, I blow him a kiss as I walk out the door.

Turning to call over my shoulder, I say, "Don't be late."

I catch a glimpse of Brooks over my shoulder, and my stomach flips. His brows push together—looking concerned. Maybe he thinks I don't trust him to show up on time with Avery, but I didn't mean it like that.

I don't have time to clear things up right now, though. I still have to meet the caterers and set up the gift bags before people start arriving. I'll talk to him about it when the party is over.

The drive from my house to the venue takes about fifteen minutes, and by the time I get there, the caterers are already in the parking lot waiting.

Tayte's here too, which is weird because he never helps with anything.

I hop out of my car and load my arms with gift bags so I don't have to make as many trips.

Tayte meets me and takes them out of my hands, freeing me up to grab more.

"What are you doing here, Uncle Tater Tot?"

He quirks a brow and smiles at me.

"This conversation feels like déjà vu."

I bump his shoulder with mine and roll my eyes.

"Speaking of—want to talk about the last time you were around for someone to call you Uncle Tater Tot?"

His eyes cut away, and he shrugs. "Not particularly."

"Fine, but we will talk about it eventually. Now, back to my original question. What are you doing here?"

"Can't a guy just come to help out his baby sister?"

"Maybe some guys, but not you. You only ever show up under suspicious circumstances. Besides, you aren't one for decorating, so I have to assume there are underlying reasons for your presence."

A dark look passes over his face, but in a second, it smooths out, and he's back to my light-hearted brother again.

"You're starting to be the favorite child with all this party planning. I need to reclaim the title." The sarcasm doesn't reach his voice, so I stop in the middle of the parking lot and shuffle some of the bags I'm holding to pull him to a stop with me.

"Hey," I say, studying his face, "are you sure you're okay?"

He plasters a bright smile on his face, but it's too big to be real.

"I'm fine, little sister. There's no need to worry about me."

There's a nagging feeling in my gut telling me I need to question him, but he takes off walking again before I can.

I follow, meeting with the caterers and opening the doors so they can start to set up, but I don't let Tayte off the hook.

"Tayte," I say, calling for his attention as we spread the round tablecloths over the tables, "tell me what's going on. I told you about me and Brooks when you asked."

He shoots me a look that says *really?* We both know I talked to him unwillingly, but I'm good at blackmail—he's the one who taught me.

"Okay, maybe I didn't *want* to talk to you, but I still did. That has to count for something."

He sighs, and his shoulders tense like they are holding the weight of the world.

"It's Mia—" he says, but he doesn't offer further details.

"What about her?" I ask. Prying information from him is like talking to my three year old.

"She drives me crazy."

A laugh bursts out of me before I can stop it, and he sends me a withering glare.

"I'm sorry—it's just—Mia is the nicest person I have ever met."

"Have you met that demon?" he asks. "She is *not* nice."

I laugh again, but this time because my big brother is hopeless.

"Tayte, by the look in your eye, I would say she drives you crazy in a

188

lot of ways, but none of them are bad."

"I don't know what you're talking about. She has a boyfriend—if he can be called that. He's a tool. The girl has no self-preservation."

"Have you tried talking to her about it?"

He shakes his head. "What is your suggestion—bake her some cookies and pop in to tell her that her boyfriend is a jerk? How neighborly of me."

I shrug, "It couldn't hurt."

He grabs another tablecloth and shakes out the wrinkles. "I don't want to talk about it anymore. I came here to help you so I could get out of my house, so let's go."

"Well, thanks for that," I say. He starts to turn away, but I put my hand on his bicep, stopping him. "Listen, as my big brother, you've always felt like you've needed to fix my life when things go wrong. I accept that because you are my big brother, and I love you. You can't do that for other people, though. That's all I'm going to say."

He sighs, and I take that to mean he agrees with me—at least, that's as close to an agreement as I will get.

"How are things with Brooks?" he asks, changing the topic.

I tried to hide the smile on my face, but there's too much happiness there.

"I'm still scared of a lot of things with Brooks, but I'm happy."

He turns back to me, eyes tracking my movements. "What are you scared of?"

"I don't know—I think I'm afraid we will fall back into the same patterns once we get comfortable again. He talks to me more than before, and we are still going to therapy, but sometimes I feel like he's still holding back—afraid to let me see all his pieces."

I look away, letting my eyes roam around the room.

"He loves you," Tayte says, touching my shoulder. "Just give him time. You both are still working this out, and that takes time."

I nod but can't help the knot of worry that stays stuck in my chest. We've always loved each other, but I need him to trust me too.

Chapter 28

Brooks

My finger taps against the steering wheel—the picture of Emryn in that black dress stuck in my head.

I should have talked to Emryn about this. I almost told her about the interview before she left. Then she smiled at me, and I didn't want to ruin this night for her with worry about me. She's worked hard to make this a good night for her parents.

I'll attend the interview, make it to the party, and tell her about it afterward. Simple as that.

"Daddy, are we going to sit in the car all night?" Avery asks.

Unbuckling my seat belt, I turn so I can see her. "We aren't. We'll get out, but you have to stay with Papaw Kip for a little while. I'll be back, and then we will go to the party, okay?"

She nods, oblivious to the worry storming through my chest.

"I love Papaw Kip. He always lets me have candy when you guys aren't looking."

I hide my eye roll by opening the truck door and getting out because of course he does.

"Come on," I say, opening her door and unbuckling her seat, "I have to hurry so I can get back. I don't want us to be late for the party."

She nods and takes my hand, following along up the sidewalk to my childhood home.

It's changed over the last few years. Kip has done a lot of updating. When I was young, the house was run down, in desperate need of a paint job, and lacked central air and heat. Bitterness slips over me, and I revel in it for a minute. I hate that he couldn't do this for my mom when she was alive. Then I look up, and Kip is waiting for us by the door. The smile on his face as he looks at Avery makes him look lighter—younger—and I remember that I promised I would try.

As we get closer, he opens the screen door and motions us in.

"Look at my dress," Avery says, handing him her jacket. She twirls around, and the hem of her dress spins with her.

She giggles and comes to a stop.

Kip kneels in front of her so that they are eye to eye.

"You look beautiful," he says.

"I know," she says, nodding in agreement. The girl has no sense of modesty.

I stand back, watching the scene unfold. There's adoration in my daughter's eyes for the man in front of her. It's a stark contrast to the uneasiness I feel in his presence. I'm working on it, though.

I've never let Kip keep Avery before, and if I'm honest with myself, I'm not sure I would be ready for this step if I weren't desperate. I need this interview.

Kip stands back up, turning his scrutiny to me.

"Thank you," he says, tears brimming his eyes.

Two simple words.

Keeping Avery means that much to him.

A small part of me feels guilty for not letting it happen before, but a bigger part realizes I had to protect my daughter, even if it meant hurting his feelings. I've never let myself trust his sobriety. I was always waiting for the other shoe to drop, but I have to start giving him a little trust. He's proved over and over again that his sobriety is here to stay.

I nod and bend down to kiss Avery on the cheek before heading to the door.

"Son."

I still cringe at the name, but I stop and turn back around to him.

"Yes?" I ask.

He has one hand in his pocket, and the other is rubbing the back of his neck. He opens his mouth like he's going to say something and closes it again. I wait for him to continue, but he shakes his head and waves me on.

I glance at my watch. I don't have time to stick around, so I wave goodbye and jog to my truck.

———————————

I look at my watch for the fifth time in less than a minute. It's fifteen minutes past the time of the scheduled interview. Ten more minutes, and I'll have to walk out of the only possible job opportunity I've had in months.

The assistant sits behind her desk on the other side of the room. When I arrived, she asked me to take a seat and has promptly ignored me since.

Frustration ripples through me, and I push out of my chair, taking long strides to get to the other side. When I'm standing in front of her desk, I clear my throat to get her attention. She glances up and then looks down at her phone, chomping her gum as she scrolls.

"May I help you?" she asks between chomps. She doesn't bother looking up when she asks. I can't believe a man like Grayson Lewis has an assistant this unprofessional. Not that I know the man, but with his level of success, you would have to assume that professionalism is required of all his employees.

I reel in the anger bubbling in my chest and put on my biggest smile. I'm sure it looks fake, but I'm barely holding on to my patience. In any other situation, I wouldn't stick around for this, but my desperation is showing because I make no move to leave.

"I was supposed to have an interview fifteen minutes ago with Mr. Lewis. Can I get an update on when that's expected to happen?"

She lifts one shoulder but still doesn't look up from the phone. I grit my teeth and take one deep breath in. When I think I might strangle her, a man steps out from the office behind her.

"Georgia," he says in a voice that leaves no room for misinterpretation.

The woman seems unbothered by the menace in his tone. She rolls her eyes and spits her gum in the trash beside her desk.

Gone is the passive woman from before, and in her place stands fire.

Her steely gaze meets mine, and there's a threat there. I'm unsure why I earned it, but I don't cowl under it. I hold my ground, squaring my shoulders and pulling myself taller. This little imp doesn't intimidate me as much as she would like to.

"That's enough, Georgia," the man says.

"Fine. It's difficult faking inability anyways," she says, shooting me one last glare.

My shoulders tense in response to her clear accusation. The dart hits directly where she intended, but I won't let her know. Sure, my company failed, but I was still a good contractor.

I don't understand why this interview has drawn her ire, but she clearly doesn't want me here.

My attention goes back to the man as the woman stomps away to the elevators, pressing the button with enough force to break the thing. There's admiration on the man's face as he watches her go, but when he notices I'm watching, he schools his features into the cool look he wore before. There's something about that look that's familiar, but I can't pinpoint why. His features aren't inherently familiar. He has dark hair and a strong nose. His beard looks several days old but well-maintained. None of those are the reasons he seems familiar, though.

It's the look. I've seen that look before, but where?

He extends his hand and steps forward, "I'm Grayson Lewis."

I shake his offered hand. I firmly believe that a handshake tells a lot about a man, and right now, Grayson's handshake tells me that I'm not at the top of his list of candidates if the force with which he grips my hand is any indication.

I don't flinch, refusing to show weakness.

I should have asked Kip more questions.

He lets go of my hand and motions for me to follow him.

We step into his office, and he takes a seat behind his desk. There are two leather chairs in front of him, and I take a seat in the one that gives me a view of the door. I want to be able to see if the assistant comes back. She might stab me in the back if given the chance.

"So, Brooks, is it?"

"Yes, thank you for the opportunity for this interview, but I have to ask—did my dad coerce you into this?"

He quirks an eyebrow and studies me. "Why would you ask that?"

"Well, I can't say this is a typical start for an interview, and the only reason I can think of for the hostility is because of my dad. So, I'll ask again—did he coerce you into this?"

"Do I look like a man that can be coerced?" he asks.

I keep my voice calm and collected as I say, "If you had asked me that before today, based on what I have heard about you, my answer would have been no, but this whole interview says otherwise."

His eyes narrow, spitting fire my way, and at that moment, it hits me that I know who he looks like. My father used to look at me the same way when I didn't give him the answer he wanted growing up.

A thought hits me, and my heart kicks up another notch.

"What's the real reason I'm here?" I ask.

The silence is loud—the sound of my heart beating in my ears as I wait for him to reveal what I already know is coming.

"Kip didn't tell you, did he?" Grayson asks.

It takes everything in me not to visibly flinch at his question. Kip sent me into this meeting blind, and I let him.

"I can't say he did, so how about you tell me instead?

His face is blank, and his voice is emotionless when he responds, saying, "I'm your big brother."

Since I entered this room, I have tried to keep my emotions in check, but sparks burn through my veins. I can't stay still any longer. I push out of the chair and pace the area in front of the desk.

Grayson stays in his chair, watching me. He leans back, stoic. He looks bored with the idea of a secret sibling while I'm drowning. He didn't get that from my dad. His emotions were always a lit fuse waiting to explode, especially when he was drinking.

I study him as I pace back and forth, wondering how I missed it when I first came in. Our hair color is the same, but that in itself isn't telling. It's the eyes. They are the same icy blue as my own. My dad—our dad—has the same.

How could I miss that?

I stop in front of his desk and push my knuckles into the wood. I need a moment to think.

My dad has a secret family. Was he cheating on my mom? Has he known about this my whole life? I pull at the roots of my hair, a million questions flitting through my mind.

I look up at Grayson, and his lips flip up in a smirk. I want to pummel his face for being so calm about this.

"Is that why you gave me the interview," I growl, anger crawling up my spine until I'm afraid I might explode.

"If I'm being honest, I was curious. I thought Kip told you about me, and you were cashing in on the success of your new big brother."

The words are a spark detonating the bomb inside of me. I slam my hand against the desk.

"I just wanted to take care of my family," I roar.

There's a bitterness in his eyes that I know well, and I realize, without a shadow of a doubt, I was never going to get this job. I was a pawn in whatever game Kip was playing this time.

I catch a glimpse of my watch, and anger is replaced with fear as it slices through my chest.

This game might have cost me a job and my family.

I won't make it to the party on time, and as much as I would love to blame Kip for all of this, I'm to blame too.

I chose to trust him, and I shouldn't have. That's on me, but more than that, I should have talked to Emryn about this interview. I should have communicated with her because, once again, I've left her out of something big. I can only pray she forgives me.

Walking out of the office, I don't look back when Grayson calls my name. I don't have time for the drama that Kip's created. If Grayson wants to reach out as my brother, I'll answer the phone, but that's all I can promise.

From what I experienced today, he is a lot more like our father than I am, and I don't need another person like that in my life. I've been made a fool of enough by the one that's already there.

Chapter 29

Emryn

Brooks and Avery aren't here.

The party started over thirty minutes ago. I've sent text after text with no response. When I call, the phone goes directly to voicemail, and I'm getting worried.

I'm giving them thirty more minutes and then calling the police.

In the meantime, I have a fake smile plastered on my face, trying to keep my mental breakdown firmly in check. I'm bad about jumping to the worst conclusion. They are probably fine and will show up any minute. I don't want to scare anyone if I don't have to—especially Mom and Dad.

I glance at the door one more time before I take the stage. I've been planning this surprise for Mom and Dad for months. Mom has wanted to renew her vows for years but never took the time to do it. When I started planning this party, I knew I wanted to help that become a reality for her. I was looking forward to it, but now it's overshadowed by the worry churning in my stomach.

I stretch my smile further, hoping it doesn't slip while I'm on the stage, then step up to the microphone.

"Can I have everyone's attention, please?"

The noise around me dies to a murmur as everyone turns their attention to me.

"Today, we celebrate two of the best people I know. They've taught me a lot in my life, but the most important lesson was how to love. Since I was six years old, they have been the definition of love for me. Today, I want to give back to them. Mom and Dad, please join me on stage?"

A chorus of applause breaks out as the two make their way to the stage. When they join me, I hug them both, holding on a minute longer than I should to take in some of their strength.

"Are you okay? Where's Avery and Brooks," Mom whispers against my ear.

"Later," I say, pulling back and making sure my smile is in place.

I turn back to the microphone and look out at the crowd.

"Mom has wanted to renew her vows for some years now, so with the help of Pastor Evert, I would like to make that happen today."

Pastor Evert stands from one of the tables in the crowd and follows a path to the stage.

I look over at Mom, and tears are brimming her eyes.

"Thank you," she mouths.

I smile back at her and step off the stage. As I return to my seat, I notice Kip slip into the back of the ballroom with Avery—a fresh round of fear blooms in my chest.

When I catch his eye, I mouth, "Where's Brooks?"

He shakes his head and shrugs. I motion him to where I'm sitting, and he takes Avery's hand to lead her through the crowd.

On stage, Pastor Evert tells a story about Mom and Dad when they were a young couple, but there's a thrumming in my ears that I can't hear over.

My husband is missing and not answering the phone. Every bad scenario runs through my head like a movie.

Kip makes it to the table and sits beside me, placing Avery on the other side.

"What's going on, Kip?" I ask.

"I don't know," he says. "Brooks had that interview tonight, and he asked me a couple of days ago if I could watch Avery. I agreed. He said he would be back before the party. When he didn't show up, I loaded Avery up, and we came here."

I shake my hand. "Wait, back up. You said he asked you a couple of days ago to watch her. Why didn't he tell me about the interview?"

"I'm sorry, Emryn. I thought you knew." He says, looking sheepish.

I close my eyes and take a deep breath. That same hurt from months ago threatens to creep in, but I can't let it—not when my husband is missing. That has to be my main focus.

I turn back to the stage, trying to fit the puzzle pieces together in my head as Mom and Dad begin to exchange vows.

Dad takes the microphone in one hand and Mom's hand in the other. He looks at her with so much love, but all I can feel is my own heart breaking.

"When I made my vows to you forty years ago," Dad says. "I was too young to know what I was promising. Today, I stand here as a man who has lived a lot of life with you. I've learned that loving you means always getting to know you. It also means loving you how you need to be loved. So, I vow to never stop getting to know you. I promise to bring you flowers, especially wild ones, because I know that makes you feel loved. When we are eighty, I promise to take you on dates, even if I have to bribe our kids to sneak us out of the nursing home. Our love is different than it was forty years ago, but I vow today that I will continue to pursue you and communicate with you so I can know what our love looks like in another forty years."

Tears slip down my face faster than I can stop them. A warm hand falls on my arm, and I don't have to turn to know it's Kip. The small act of comfort is unexpected. I turn to him, and he opens his arms for me to fall into.

It's that moment that breaks me. Silent sobs wrack my body as I let my head fall to his shoulder. He wraps his arms around me in the same way my dad would.

I never expected this tonight. It was supposed to be filled with joy—not fear and betrayal.

"Emryn—" Kip says.

I look up at him, but he's looking at the door behind me.

I twirl in my seat and find Brooks standing there, looking at Kip, and his face is filled with enough anger to kill.

Brooks descends upon our seats in a fury.

I motion for Tayte, who is sitting a few tables over, to watch Avery as I pull Kip up from his seat and take hold of Brooks's arm, leading them both to the hallway.

I have no idea what's going on, but I won't let either of them ruin the party.

My whole body shakes as I open the door, and we step out.

As the door closes behind us, Brooks rips his arm out of my hold and shoves Kip against the wall. His fist is drawn, ready to strike.

"You knew what would happen when you sent me to that interview, didn't you?" he spits.

I step in front of Kip, placing myself between him and Brooks, but he doesn't let go of the lapels of Kip's jacket. The tension in my body keeps building and building. I'm on the brink of implosion.

"Brooks, what's going on?" I ask.

He flicks his gaze to me, but only for a moment.

We are in another situation where he can't be bothered to talk to me, and I'm sick of it.

I shove at his chest, but he's like a brick wall, unyielding in more ways than one.

"Let's talk about this, Son," Kip says from behind me.

Brooks's face morphs from anger to absolute fury. His teeth are barred, and the muscles jump in his jaw.

"You had ample opportunities to talk to me before tonight. You could have even talked to me tonight before I left, but you said nothing."

I'm tired of being ignored—left out of conversations I should be included in. That's the only explanation for what I do next.

There's a crack in the air as my hand connects with his cheek. I immediately feel the sting against my palm and cradle it against my chest—red blooms across Brooks's face.

For a moment, he sits there stunned. He lets go of Kip's jacket and steps back—eyes trained on me. The shock melts from his face, leaving no emotion behind. The blankness of his stare scares me.

He huffs out a laugh, but there's no mirth behind it. It's dry and humorless.

"You want to be included, Emryn? Fine, here it is. We are drowning in bills, but I didn't want you to know. I've been killing myself to find a job for our family, all while trying to save our marriage. Then Kip told me about this interview. It turns out Daddy dearest here had a secret motive for setting it up, though, and like a fool, I believed he was trying to change. He was too cowardly to tell me the real reason."

"Which is what, Brooks? What's the real reason?"

"I'm not talking about it right now."

I throw my hands up in the air.

"Of course you aren't because when do you ever talk about anything with me? Just talk to me, *please*," I beg.

I reach out involuntarily to touch his arm. It's like second nature to comfort him, but I'm torn between wanting to comfort him and letting my anger win. He promised to communicate with me. I shouldn't have to beg for that, and I don't know what it means for our marriage that I do.

He shakes his head and pulls his arm back, refusing my touch.

"I can't—not right now."

My heart physically aches in my chest.

I let my hand fall, and Brooks turns back to Kip.

"Whatever relationship that was starting to form here is done," Brooks says.

Kip opens his mouth to respond, but Brooks cuts him off. "Leave because I don't want to hear anything you have to say."

Silent tears slip down Kip's face, but he doesn't make another motion to defend himself. My brain buzzes with all the questions I have. I should step in and make Kip stay because if Brooks won't talk to me about what's going on, he needs to talk to someone, but I can't because I'm frozen—stuck wondering if it will always be this way.

Chapter 30

Brooks

Kip walks out the door without another word. I thought the knot in my stomach would loosen after I confronted him, but it's still there, pulling tighter and tighter.

Emryn is beside me, and when I turn to look at her, a fissure begins to form in my chest. The look she wears can only be described as defeat.

I put that look there, and once again, I've failed her as her husband. She needs me to talk to her, but I can't—not here. I need time to process what happened tonight.

"I'm going to go," she says, tears edging her eyes, but she doesn't leave. She stands there waiting for me to give her the one thing she needs from me.

Realization rips through me. I'm going to lose her because of this. I can see it in the way she holds herself—arms around her center, holding together all the broken pieces I created.

I step towards her, arm outstretched, but she flinches away.

My marriage is crumbling, and I'm the only one left to blame.

I open my mouth to spill my heart at her feet, but I can't force out the words she wants her to hear. They're stuck in my throat.

I see it the moment that she accepts my silence.

"I have to get back to the party," Emryn whispers.

"Just wait, please. Let's talk about something else. Just give me a minute," I beg.

A maniacal laugh rips through her lips—it's jaded. I watch her, afraid she'll run if I move toward her.

"What else do you want to talk about, Brooks? Oh, I know. Let's talk about how I was worried you were dead on the side of the road somewhere, or how about we talk about the interview I didn't even know you were going to." Anger blooms across her face, but she doesn't let up. "That's right, you didn't want to talk about that either. So, how about I talk, and you listen since I'm the only one who seems to talk anyway."

I clench my teeth to physically stop myself from interrupting her. Maybe if she gets out all the hurt and spews the anger that she needs to, she will be calm enough to hear my side. I *need* her to hear my side.

"You promised," she says, her voice breaking. A crack forms in my chest, one more shot away from breaking. "You promised that we would be a team—that you would talk to me, but how many things have you been keeping from me? The bills, the interview, and now whatever happened at that interview to make you so mad. You think you have to do everything on your own, but you don't."

"I do, Emryn," I yell. "I do because I always have. Even now, I can see you pulling away because I can't give you what you need."

She shakes her head, "All I need, Brooks, is for you to talk to me."

"I can't, Emryn. I don't want pity—not yours or your dad's. I don't want it," I yell.

My chest heaves as I try to gain control of all the things falling apart around me.

I see her light dim when she finally accepts what I'm saying.

"Dad didn't offer you a job out of pity. He did it because he loves you, and so do I. You see it as a weakness, but really, it's just your pride. There, for a moment, I thought things would change. You gave me a peek inside, but you'll always resort back to hiding yourself."

That's the third shot, and my heart splits wide open.

"That's not fair," I choke out.

She looks at me with the pity I never wanted from her.

"No, what's not fair is that I feel like I'm begging for something I'm losing. Figure out what you want, Brooks, and I'll do the same. Right now, you need to leave because I have a party to get back to. Go home," she says, turning and walking towards the door.

"Are you coming home tonight?" There's fear in my voice when I ask. I'm scared that she will leave again and this time she won't return.

She stops but doesn't look at me when she answers. "I'll be there later because I refuse to disrupt our daughter's life again. Not today, at least. I'll sleep in the guest room. Don't wait up on us."

At that, she walks through the door—away from me.

She's coming home, but I don't want to leave here without her knowing how much I love her. I let her walk out of my life one time. I'm not doing it again. Maybe I didn't chase her when she left before, but I won't make that same mistake twice.

I sling open the door, determined to catch up with her.

Music plays when I enter the ballroom, and guests are on the dance floor. Tayte is twirling Avery around.

I spot Emryn beside the stage. Tears stream down her face as she tries to catch her breath and talk to her mom.

My soul is tethered to hers—everything in me pulls me to her.

When I step that way, a hand falls on my shoulder, stopping me.

Jonathan's hand tightens as I try to escape his grip.

He shakes his head, "Not here. You need to give her time. Let her calm down a minute."

I look him in the eye because I respect this man, but I can't do what he's asking me, "Respectfully, sir, I can't do that, so I'm going to ask you to let go of my arm while I go speak to my wife."

I try again to step away from him, but this time, when I turn around, Tayte is standing there.

He must have seen Emryn crying and Jonathan holding onto my arm while dancing with Avery. I look for her because I don't want her in the middle of this. I spot her on the edge of the dance floor. She's still twirling around, darting in and out of the people dancing.

"Is there a problem here?" Tayte asks.

"There won't be if you mind your own business," I growl. I have nothing against Tayte in normal circumstances, but he's standing between me and my wife.

I'll run through him if I have to.

Tayte squares his shoulders, readying himself to block my path.

Jonathan's voice comes from behind me.

"Brooks, listen to me. If you go over there right now, it's only going to make things worse. We are in a party full of people—a party she's worked hard to put together. Don't humiliate her by making a scene."

I'm torn. I promised myself I wouldn't let Emryn walk away again, but Jonathan is right—if I go over there and demand that she talk to me, it will cause a scene. I don't want to do that to her. She doesn't deserve it.

She didn't deserve anything that happened tonight.

"Fine. I'll leave and give her time, but I won't lose her. You make sure she knows that I'm going to fight for her. I'll see her at home."

He claps my back and gives me a hint of a smile, "I wouldn't expect anything less, Son."

Just like with my dad, those words dig their way into the hole standing wide open in my chest. Jonathan has said that word to me a hundred times before, but what Emryn said earlier about him offering me the job because he loves me makes it stick.

"Do you really see me that way, sir?" I ask. I can hear the broken boy of my past in my voice when I ask the question. I've tried to bury him, but he's always there, lingering below the surface.

"Since you were six years old and asked me for my daughter's hand in marriage."

————————————

As I walk out the venue doors, my heart screams to turn back around and get my wife. There's a pull to her that I have to fight against—telling myself to put one foot in front of the other.

Cool air fills my lungs, and I welcome the sting because the rest of me is numb—until I see a man leaning up against my truck.

Walking past him, I dig my keys out of my pocket to unlock my truck door, refusing to look at him.

"Brooks, wait."

"What, Kip? What do you want from me? Because I'll be honest, I have nothing left to give."

He looks down at the ground and kicks a rock with the toe of his boot.

"I know you asked me to leave, and I will, but not before I tell you I loved your mother very much. She was the best woman I've ever had the pleasure of loving."

I don't have it in me to fight anymore, not tonight.

"Why are you telling me this?" I ask.

"Because I know that was probably one of the first questions you had when you found out about Grayson, but I never cheated on your mother. She and I started dating a year before you were born. We were married two months after we started dating, and then ten months later, we had you."

"Oh yeah? Then where does Grayson come in?" I ask sardonically.

He ignores my tone and continues, "Grayson is older than you. A few years before your mother and I started dating, I had a girlfriend, but I was drinking too much even then. She left town without a goodbye. I didn't know about him. She never told me, and I don't blame her. I wasn't good for him. I wasn't good for you, but you took the brunt of it. I'm sorry for that."

Sorry.

He's sorry. The thought is laughable because even now, I'm taking the brunt of his toxicity.

"Maybe I could believe that apology if you hadn't sent me in blind tonight. You had every chance to tell me, and you didn't. Typical Kip—never owning up to his mistakes."

His head snaps up to look at me.

"You think I didn't tell you because I'm ashamed?" His voice is as hard as steel.

"If the shoe fits," I say, unbothered.

"You listen to me. I have a lot of regrets in my life, but my kids are not one of them. I failed you, and your brother for that matter, but from the day you were born, and the day I found out about Grayson, I have been proud of you both. I didn't tell you because I didn't want to jeopardize any chance of fixing my relationship with you."

"So what did you expect to happen when I went there tonight? Did you think that it wouldn't come up?"

He shoves his hand in his hair, pulling tight at the roots.

"I don't know, Brooks. I don't know what I thought. All I knew was that you were losing your family over a job, and I didn't want that for you. I called Grayson about an interview, and he agreed. That was probably a mistake too, because he doesn't want much to do with me either, so maybe I thought he wouldn't mention it."

"How did that turn out for you," I huff.

"Not very well," he sighs, resigned.

I take a moment to look at him. He's aged a lot—years of drinking will do that to you—but underneath that, there's a clearness to his skin that I haven't ever seen. His cheeks are no longer sunken like when I was young, but sadness haunts his eyes. I could continue to hold my past against him, but it's like holding on to a grenade—it won't just hurt him when it explodes.

I lean against my truck and slide down until I'm sitting on the ground.

"Thank you for keeping Avery and bringing her here tonight," I say. He's tried these past few years. I've seen him try, but I refused to acknowledge it. The fact that he brought Avery here tonight after I didn't show up says a lot. I might not like his choice to keep me in the dark about Grayson, but I didn't make it easy for him to tell me either.

His mouth is open as he gapes at me. He clears his throat before saying, "You're welcome."

I lean my head against the truck. The asphalt is cold through my pants, but my energy seeps out. I don't have it in me to get up.

Kip sits on the ground beside me and looks up, mirroring my position.

"I'm sorry about what happened back there with Emryn."

"Yeah, me too. Turns out, I have a lot of regrets too."

He rolls his head toward me and studies me.

"Is there something I can do to help?"

It's on the tip of my tongue to tell him he's already done enough, but I hold back.

"No. I don't think there is."

He nods but doesn't look away.

"Don't let her slip through your fingers, Brooks. There are a lot of things I would tell your mom if I had the chance. I'll never get that chance, but you will. Don't take that for granted."

"She doesn't want anything to do with me right now, and I don't blame her. I broke promises that I said I wouldn't."

His hand falls on the back of my head.

"She'll come around, Son. She'll come around."

210

Chapter 31

Emryn

"Emryn," Mom says my name from beside me.

When I left Brooks in the hallway, I ran straight to her arms. This whole thing feels like a repeat of the day I walked away from him in our kitchen months ago. I wanted to believe we were past this, but nothing has changed.

He still can't communicate with me, and I'm left to decide what that means for our marriage.

"Yes?" I ask.

The noise from the party starts to dissipate as people begin to leave. I'm ready for this whole night to be over. A headache is forming in the back of my neck, and I can't stand the thought of one more person asking me where Brooks went.

"Your dad and I are about to head out. Do you need any help with the cleanup before we go?" she asked, looking concerned.

"No, the caterers are cleaning up their part. I just have to take down the decorations. I'll recruit Tayte to stay and help with that. Can you take Avery home with you, though? She's getting pretty tired."

"Of course, we can. You don't have to ask." She pats my cheek, and I look over to my daughter, who has her head on the table. Her eyelids open and close slower each time she blinks.

She must overhear me because she raises her head and says, "I'm not

211

tired, Mommy. I can dance all night."

Her mouth opens in a yawn, and I smile at her, wondering if her life will be disrupted again because Brooks and I can't figure out how to make this work.

"Oh yeah, party girl, you don't seem tired at all," I say, smoothing her hair back from her face. "How about this—you go with Grandpa and Grandma tonight, and when I pick you up tomorrow, we can pick pumpkins at the pumpkin patch."

"Yes," she squeals.

Mom moves to pick Avery up. Then she stops and turns back to me, gathering me in her arms and squeezing tight.

"It's all going to be okay, sweet girl. Pray about it," she says before letting me go and returning to collecting Avery.

I watch as they walk away, Mom carrying Avery in her arms and Avery waving over her shoulder. They walk over to where my dad is standing in the corner, and his lips tip up as he watches them approach. He leans down and takes Avery from Mom, but not before placing a sweet kiss against Mom's cheek. Her face lights up, and my heart breaks a little more.

Brooks and I are not going to be them. Our problems are bigger than just forgetting to date. For us, it's always, "We'll talk later," but this time, I don't know that there will be a later.

During our time apart, I worked on myself. I changed, and I tried to communicate. When I wanted to go to school, I told him. I didn't leave him in the dark about my plans.

Tonight, something big happened, and I was the last to know—again. As his wife, shouldn't I be the first person he wants to talk to?

I turn away from my parents, unable to handle the sight of their love right now. That's all I've ever wanted for Brooks and me, but I can't force it.

I concentrate on pulling the centerpieces from the table and placing them in a pile to be put in the car later.

A few people come over to say their goodbyes, and I force a polite goodbye each time.

When I'm at the last table, Mrs. Evert steps into my view.

"Emmie girl, let's take a walk."

She motions for me to follow. My body rages at the idea of having to carry on a conversation while pain splits me from the inside, but my Southern manners win out.

"Yes, ma'am," I say, placing the decor I hold in a pile with the others.

She walks to the other side of the venue, and I follow at her pace, keeping an eye on her as we walk. She's getting older, and as lively as she may be with hair that's red today, it doesn't take away the problems of old age. Her gait is slow and uneven, but still, she perseveres.

When we reach the hallway that Brooks and I stood in earlier, she stops and sits on the bench beside the door.

She is quiet long enough to take her seat, and then she doesn't hold back her punches. Subtlety isn't her middle name—I shouldn't have expected anything less.

"What's got you look so doom and gloom tonight, girl?" she asks.

"Nothing. I'm just tired. This event took a lot of work." Only part of that is a lie. I am tired, but not from the party.

The look she throws me is scathing.

"Now, don't lie to me. I love you too much for that. I can't help but notice your husband isn't here."

"Yeah—you and everyone else," I mumble. I'm a teenager again, with all the attitude of a girl with a broken heart.

"What was that? Speak up. I'm getting old, and my hearing is going."

"We had a disagreement," I say, this time a little louder.

"A disagreement, huh? What about?" she asks.

"What it's always about. I begged him to talk to me, and he did the opposite."

"Hmm," she hums. "And how did you respond to this disagreement?"
Shame fills my cheeks because I already know where this is going.
"Probably not very well. But—in my defense, I tried to talk to him. I
gave him a chance to communicate, but he wouldn't, and I can't force
him."

"Emryn, I'm going to fill you in on a little secret." Her eyes twinkle
with mischief that always lays just below the surface. "Men are dense."

An unexpected laugh bubbles out.

"There's my girl," Mrs. Evert says. "Now, I will tell you the rest of
the story. Men might be dense, but women are too. We aren't perfect,
but we fill the gaps where the other is missing."

"So, what? I shouldn't have gotten angry?" I ask. I pace the hallway
in front of her—back and forth. Tears burn my throat.

"I'm so sick of crying," I say in a voice clogged with emotion as I wipe
the back of my hand under my eyes.

She watches my outburst but doesn't say anything. She lets me pace
and pace until, finally, the words spill out.

"Something big happened tonight. I could tell it in the way he held
himself when he walked in. Then, he got into a fight with Kip. He's
never done that before—no matter how far Kip's pushed him. I begged
him to talk to me—to let me in, but he didn't. I'm just so tired." I slump
into the seat beside her and tilt my head against the wall to stare at the
ceiling. If I fixate on one spot, hoping it will hold the tears at bay until
I get home.

"Did it occur to you that maybe he needed to process whatever
happened?

I roll my head, so I'm looking at her now.

She continues, "He's different from you. He needs time to process—
most men do. God made him that way—on purpose. He didn't make
a mistake when he made Brooks. He didn't make a mistake when he
made you, either. He just made you both different."

"Maybe I could believe that if Brooks hadn't tried hiding everything in the past. He was too proud to talk to me then, so why would that be different now?"

"Are you the same person you were two months ago or even last week?"

I let my hands go limp beside me. She's right. I'm not the same person I was a few months ago. I've grown and learned from our mistakes.

Tonight doesn't have to define our marriage, but I can't guarantee it won't—and that scares me. I can give Brooks the time he needs to process. It's the only thing left I have to give him. Everything else is on him, and that leaves me where I was before—broken.

An hour later, the venue is quiet, and everyone has left except for Tayte and me.

We work in silence, folding tablecloths and packing away the decor into boxes.

I catch him throwing pointed glances my way, but I ignore it. It's killing him to keep his mouth shut.

"Do you want me to punch him?" he asks after five more minutes of silence. He might have exploded if he had gone any longer.

I shrug my shoulder and answer with a muted "No."

He expected me to laugh, but I can't—not right now.

"I'm worried about you, Emryn."

"I'm fine," I say, but even my ears are unconvinced.

I'm as far away from fine as a person can be.

The door to the kitchen creaks open, and the caterer steps out.

"We need someone to sign for the bill."

I look at Tayte, and he nods.

When the door closes behind him, I realize maybe I should have been the one that went. I'm alone for the first time since the fight, and my thoughts are louder than the silence.

It's unnerving how they fill the quiet and add to my headache.

Even after talking to Mrs. Evert, this burden lies heavy on my shoulders, pulling me down until my knees hit the floor.

There's a visceral need thrumming through my veins, calling me to lay it all out at his feet—to let go of the pain lodged like a thorn inside my chest.

"Please, God," I beg. The words slip from my lips—jagged and raw. I don't know what it is I'm praying for.

Maybe it's for him to pull out the thorn before it festers, or perhaps I'm begging him to surround my husband with the comfort I can't offer him. Maybe it's both.

My hands fall open to my sides, offering it all to him. All the pain—my marriage, our future—lies in his hands. I can't hold on to it anymore. It's slipping through my fingers like quicksand.

I repeat the words, letting the brokenness flow out of me.

It's not a prayer of substance. It's desperate and lost.

My body rocks back and forth, calling for him to fill my soul with him.

There's no reason for him to hear my call. I don't deserve it.

Awareness rattles through me.

I don't deserve it.

This past year, I let my relationship with God fall further down my list. I tried to sort life out on my own—relying on myself to fix the fissures—but even when I pushed him away, he stood there waiting for me to figure out that I couldn't do it alone.

He loved me enough to let me process before I ran to him.

Chapter 32

E mryn,

I'm sorry.

Love,

Brooks.

Chapter 33

B rooks,
   I heard you when you said you couldn't talk to me. I shouldn't
   have pushed.

I want to be the person you need, the wife you need, and I want to know
all of you—the good and the bad.

Tonight, I realized that for me to know you, I have to give you grace.

You deserve that, you know—grace and love and patience. You deserve all
the good things because you are a good man.

I'm not sure you know that, but you are—one of the best.

I can picture you reading this letter, shaking your head at the last part
because somehow you've got this idea that you have to work for the love you
receive from the people in your life.

That's not true, and none of the brokenness you try to hide from the world
will change that.

You don't have to earn your worthiness because you are already worthy.

You're a great dad, and even at our worst point, you were still a good
husband because your intentions were good. I believe that intentions matter—
they are a look into a person's soul.

Your soul is beautiful and fragile—not in a bad way, but in a way that
makes you protect it.

I'm sorry for not recognizing what you needed from me tonight.

I understand now that you need time to process whatever happened, but *please, Brooks, don't shut me out forever.*

Love,
Emryn

Chapter 34

Brooks

A dull thump resounds in my chest as I read the words over and over again.

I left a note for Emryn to find when she got home last night because I wanted to give her the space she asked for. She deserved that much. When I woke up this morning, she was already gone—giving me the space I thought I was giving to her.

Placing the note down, I pull my phone out of my pocket. It's heavy in my hand, leaden with the weight of the phone call I know I have to make.

With slow movements, my thumb swipes across the screen until I find the number I'm looking for. Last night made it clear that I have issues I can't deal with alone. I may have chosen to listen to my dad after the party, but my resentment keeps creeping up each time he messes up. It runs deeper than my ability to heal—at least by myself, and my family deserves to have me healed.

The phone rings until finally, Dr. Phelps picks up, and an hour later, I find myself sitting on the couch that I despised just months before, picking at the same fraying thread.

Dr. Phelps stares at me with patience clear on his face, waiting for me to give him something—anything—but the words are clogged in my throat.

Why is talking so hard? It's simply stringing words together, but in the moments I need to, my throat constricts around them.

The older man doesn't attempt to fill the room with babble but instead sits and lets me gather my thoughts.

Pressure builds inside until the words pour out of my mouth like water flowing out of a broken dam.

"I have a brother," I blurt.

He raises one eyebrow, but I rush forward. If I don't get it all out to this one person, I'm not sure I ever will. I have to start somewhere.

"My dad set up an interview, which should have been strange to me. The man has been self-serving my whole life. I was desperate. I needed a job—for my family—for me. I felt useless without work, so I went. It was the same day as Emryn's parents' anniversary party. I thought I could go to the interview, get back in time for the party, and then tell Emryn all about it. I wanted to surprise her, but the interview was awful, and my dad was at the party when I arrived. I was angry at everything, so when she begged me to talk to her, I couldn't."

Dr. Phelps holds up his hand, and his face turns contemplative. "Did *really* you want to surprise her?"

I shake my head in confusion, "What do you mean? I just told you I did."

"Brooks, you and Emryn have been coming to me for several months. I've seen you both grow a lot during that time, but in my time as a therapist, I've learned to sit back and read the things people don't say, so tell me, what's the real reason you didn't tell Emryn about the interview before?"

A lump forms in my throat because he's right. I tried convincing myself that I wanted to surprise Emryn with the interview, but I was really falling back into old habits. I didn't talk to her because I felt inadequate. Emryn came home from her meeting, and I was staring at a pile of unpaid bills. She was happy, and I feared bursting that bubble for her.

"Emryn applied for school. She had a meeting a couple of weeks ago, and when she came home. She glowed. She was so happy. I didn't want her to feel like I was taking school away from her. She quit when we were younger because we got married, and I started my business. We had a family. It was never the right time for her. I want this to be the right time for her. She told me once that she felt like she lost herself. I don't want her to ever feel like that again."

"How would this interview have made her feel that way?" he asks, his brows pulling together.

"She would have felt like she needed to take care of me. It's who she is. She takes care of people, but before, I was too blind to see that when she does, she doesn't take care of herself."

"Did you ever stop to think that she won't allow herself to be in that place again either? She can love you and love herself too. It doesn't have to be all or nothing."

My hands are still against the fray on the couch. "I messed up, didn't I?"

There's a twinkle in his eye as he looks at me now, "We are all human. We mess up, but it's how we fix our messes that matter. So—let's talk about how we can fix this. You need some strategies that will help you in the times when you feel you struggle to communicate. How have the letters worked for you?"

I lean back against the couch, sinking into the plushness of the cushions, "I guess, for me, it's made it easier to tell her how I'm feeling."

"Why do you think it's hard to talk to her outside of those letters?"

I take a minute to think about what he's asking. "I guess because I don't have to worry about her response when I write. When I'm standing there face to face with her, I worry about tainting her view of me."

His brow scrunches in confusion, "Why would her view of you be tainted?"

"Even though we grew up together, we lived two different lives. She was protected from life, and I was thrown in head first. I tried to hide that part of me from her for as long as possible. She knew my dad was an alcoholic and that we were poor, but she only saw me persevere through that. I didn't let her see the boy who cried himself to sleep every night for months when his mom died or the man who felt inadequate because he let his business, which was meant to support his family, fail. I was afraid if I let her see those versions of me because it would change her view of me."

"Let me ask you a question, Brooks. Do you think that love has to be earned?"

I tilt my head in confusion. To me, the question is silly. "Of course it does."

"I think we've found the root of our problem. Brooks, love does not have to be earned, and I can preach that to you until I'm blue in the face. Until you let someone close enough to prove that, though, things are not going to change for you. Start small. I want you to write three more letters, and I want you to tell your wife three things about you that she doesn't know. Don't take the easy way out on this. Make it deep. Let her see all of you—even the scariest parts—and then see if she still loves you."

"But what if she doesn't?"

He shrugs like that possibility wouldn't wreck my entire world, then says, "I think you will be surprised."

On the drive home, Dr. Phelps's words keep running through my mind, and instead of taking a right to turn on the street that takes me home, I find myself going straight to a house that hasn't felt like home since my mom died.

I pull into the driveway, and the front door opens as I step out of my truck. Kip stands on the porch barefooted with jeans and a t-shirt. To an outsider, he looks like a man who has his life together, but to me, he's the reason I have to fight so hard to let my wife love me. He's the root of my definition of love, and I'm learning how skewed that version is.

"Brooks, is everything okay?" he asks.

"It will be," I say, stepping onto the porch.

"Is it Emryn or Avery?" he asks, panic lacing his voice, and I realize that this man in front of me is not the same one I grew up with. Five years ago, he would have been too drunk to care about anyone but himself, but now love flits through his voice when he asks about Emryn and Avery. I've been too angry to let myself see that he has changed.

He should have told me about Grayson being my brother before the interview, but I wouldn't have listened to him even if he had tried.

"They are fine. I'm here for me. Can we sit?" I ask, pointing at the rocking chairs on the other side of the short porch.

He nods and follows me until we sit side by side, rocking in silence like we did a few weeks ago.

"Dad," I start. His head yanks in my direction, and tears glimmer in his eyes, but he remains silent, waiting for me to finish. "Why didn't you come to Mom's funeral?"

Of all the ways he's ever let me down, that one was the hardest to understand. He told me the other night that he loved my mom, but if he loved her, why didn't he come?"

"I was there." His voice is rough when he says it—pain threaded in with the words. "I sat in the back."

"I didn't see you," I argue.

He leans forward and places his hands on his knees. His head hangs down, and the tears that glimmered in his eyes before free fall onto the ground. "I didn't want you to see me. I had just come off a three-day binge. I was sober enough to know where I was but not sober enough that you couldn't smell it on me. When I walked into the church, you were sitting with the Bennett family, and I made the only selfless choice I've ever made—I let you be. You didn't deserve to deal with me drunk at your momma's funeral."

I swallow hard against the knot in my throat, but I'm not sure what to say. This whole time, I've painted this man as the villain in my life, and I won't deny that in parts of it, he was, but he loved me enough to protect me that day. As a kid—I wouldn't have recognized that he was protecting me, but as an adult, I can understand that he was doing it the best way he knew how.

"Can I ask you another question?"

He doesn't lift his head but answers me anyway. "I think you are entitled to ask me a million questions."

"Why wasn't I enough for you to get sober?" I hate how small I sound when I ask him, but I want to know. I *need* to know.

"Kid, it was never about you. I was weak. That's all there is to it. Life beat me down too many times, and I let it. But—I will tell you this. I have loved you since the day you wrapped your finger around mine in the hospital."

"I felt like I had to earn that love from you, and nothing I did was ever good enough to earn it," I admit.

"I'm sorry I couldn't show you what love is supposed to look like. You never had to earn it. You've always had it. I've just never been good at showing it."

Growing up, I never thought I would have anything in common with my dad, but this is it. Neither of us knows how to love or let someone love us.

It's time I break that generational curse, though.

"I'm sorry for not letting you show me the last couple of years."

"It's okay, Son. You had every right to be angry with me. I wasn't a great dad, but I'm trying to change."

"I know, and I promise to make that easier on you from now on."

He nods and changes the subject. "How are things with Emryn? Have you told her about Grayson yet?"

I shake my head, "We haven't talked since last night. She had already left when I got up this morning."

"Take it from me, Brooks. Regret is an awful thing to live with. Let people love you and show them that you love them back."

I stand up and walk over to the edge of the porch. My back is to my dad, but I can feel his eyes on me.

"I think the same goes for you too, Dad. I know I didn't make it easy for you to tell me about Grayson, but maybe one day, we will find ourselves in a place where we can tell each other things—and maybe that will include Grayson too."

"I hope so, Son. I hope so."

Chapter 35

E mryn,
    I messed up with you—again. I should have talked to you, but
    sometimes the words I want to say get clogged in my throat—no
matter how hard I try, they won't come out.

I will work on that, but I need you to know that it has never been because
of you.

Growing up, I didn't have the kind of support you did. It was only me. I
had to take care of myself—and, before she died, my mom. No one's ever
just taken care of me. It's ingrained in me to handle things alone because it's
what I've always done.

I promised to rely on you—to let you in—but when it came time to do that,
I let you down. So, I'll make you a different promise. I promise to work on
it, and if I can't speak the words, I promise to write you a letter.

So here's my first letter:

I have a brother.

That night of your parents' anniversary party, I had an interview that
my dad set up. I took it out of desperation. I wanted to fix things before you
knew how much I had screwed up our lives. I didn't want you to look at me
like my mom did my dad. So, I called and set it up. I figured if it went well,
I could surprise you, and if I didn't get it, no harm, no foul. I could just keep
looking.

I went to the interview, but I wasn't prepared to find out I had a brother, *and Grayson, that's his name, thought I was only there because I was trying to mooch off him.*

For the first time in my life, I felt like my dad.

Here's this man in front of me who has worked for everything he has, and I'm practically begging him for a job. I know the circumstances aren't the same. I am qualified for the position, but he didn't know that. He only knew that "family" came out of the woodwork, asking him for something. I know how that feels, so I left, but not without a lot of regrets.

Not only did I walk out without a job, but I was also late for the party.

If I thought I was desperate before walking into that meeting, it was nothing compared to how I felt walking out of it—facing the fact that I had let you down again, and the task of looking through one more job posting made me physically ill.

I left and went to pick up Avery from Kip, but she wasn't there. Panic overtook me when I couldn't find our daughter. I tried calling Kip a hundred times as I headed to you, but he didn't answer. All I could think about was getting to you so we could find our daughter, but when I got to the party, and Kip was sitting beside you, it was like the volcano bubbling just below the surface finally erupted.

I wanted to talk to you that night, but I couldn't. I couldn't even wrap my head around everything that seemed to happen at once, let alone talk to you about them.

This is me telling you now, though, and hoping it's not too late because you're my family. My dad and I—well— we are working on it, and my brother, I'm not sure what will happen there. I hope one day I can get to know him, but you—you, I can't live without. You're my best friend.

Love,

Brooks

Chapter 36

E mryn,
Finances. *That's another area I haven't been open with you about because it's also another place where our backgrounds are different.*

I grew up poor, Emryn—really poor. I know that you saw some of that, but I tried to hide a lot of it from you.

I NEVER let you come to my house, especially in the winter, because I wasn't sure there would be heat. You didn't have to worry about that, and I'm glad you didn't. It made us different, though.

When we got married, I wanted you to have the lifestyle that you were used to, so anytime you asked, I never said no. I just worked harder. I thought if I told you no, it would be like me telling you that I couldn't provide for you. As a man—especially with a dad like mine—it hurt my pride.

Here's the truth about where we are. I need you to brace yourself because it is ugly. Unless I find a job soon, we will lose a lot more than just my business. I've applied for hundreds of jobs, but they haven't amounted to anything. Then I received that job offer from your dad. Even with things going from bad to worse with our finances, I couldn't make myself take it.

Your dad has been the only role model I have ever had in my life, and a lot of things became clear to me the night of your parents' party. You said I see love as a weakness, but that's only partially true. I don't feel weak when I love you, but it makes me feel weak to receive love.

I'm afraid of being the boy I was after my mom died, begging someone to love him enough to provide basic necessities. I can't ever be that boy again, so I built an armor around me, not realizing what I had experienced wasn't love. I've pushed away people who wanted to show me what true love is. But—you're all still here, waiting for me to realize that love isn't conditional.

I've thought about it a lot, and I'm going to take the job offer from your dad. It no longer feels like pity—but love. I'm not saying I won't struggle later. I think I'll have to always remind myself that pity and love are not the same emotion, but I hope I'll have you there to help me work through it when I start to feel that way again.

Love,
Brooks

Chapter 37

Emryn,

When we were on our date, you asked me about my dreams. I told you that you are my dream. That's true, but it's more than that.

I want everything with you. I want this life we built and our little girl to know love because of how we love each other. I want her to have a sibling to play with—maybe two or three of them—but most of all, I want to watch them grow up while we grow old together.

For so long, I've been afraid to dream of those things. I've loved you most of my life, even before I realized what love was. Well, I guess I'm still learning what love is. Despite that, I've always held myself back a little. I was afraid—terrified—of everything disappearing out from under me, and then you left. It was my worst nightmare come true. I'm not blaming you because I know the part I played in causing that, but, in a way, it confirmed my fear.

Despite how much work we've put in over the last couple of months, I still secretly harbored the fear that I'll mess up one day, and then you won't come back. So, when tensions were high at the anniversary party, all I could think about was if I let you in, then you decided to leave anyway, my heart wouldn't be able to take it.

I made the wrong choice. I should have trusted you because you deserve my trust. You've earned it many times over throughout the years.

These letters are my way of letting you see me, all of me, and I guess it's my way of asking if you still want to make dreams come true with me.

Love,
 Brooks

Chapter 38

Emryn

Tears stream down my face as I read each letter over and over. I let the words seep into my soul, healing every crack and fracture formed over the last year. Brooks isn't perfect, but he's trying, and effort is all I've ever needed from him.

The night of the party, he scared me. Flashes of lonely nights and miscommunication ran through my mind as I stood there begging him to talk—about anything.

The letters I hold in my hand prove that Mrs. Evert was right. Brooks isn't me. He needs time to process. It doesn't mean that we will revert to old habits again. We've both grown. I have to trust him.

I look absentmindedly around the kitchen, wondering where my husband is. He got home late last night. I had been in the guest room again, but he didn't seek me out. Early this morning, I heard the front door open, but I was still half asleep. When I finally woke up enough to come downstairs, he was gone. I found the letters on the kitchen counter when I went to start breakfast.

My heart aches for everything he's been shouldering—feelings of inadequacy, finances, his brother.

He has a brother.

I should have handled the night of the party better—loved him the way he needed to be loved.

A knock at the front door jars me. I fold the letters and place them back down on the counter. When I reach the hallway, I look down to the front door where Kip Montgomery stands on the other side.

Emotions run through me as I walk down the hall—gratefulness for taking care of Avery the other night, pity because he has a son he never knew about, and anger because, once again, he let Brooks down.

He nods at me when I open the door, and I usher him in without a word.

"Kip," I say once we are standing in the living room, "Brooks isn't here right now. I don't know when he will be back, but I can call him and see if he will answer."

His lips have a slight uptick—a smirk that looks so much like the one Brooks wears when he finds something funny. I'm not sure where the joke is, but I feel like the butt of it. I wrap my arms around my stomach as unease fills me.

Kip watches my motions, and his face softens.

"Can we sit a minute?" he asks, tilting his head towards the couch. His voice is hesitant, and I realize that he's nervous. He holds a ball cap, flattening and straightening the brim repeatedly.

"Sure," I say.

He takes a seat on the loveseat, and I sit on the couch next to him, waiting for the reason he is here.

"How's Avery?"

My brows dip. Is that why he's here—to talk about Avery? He's never stopped in like this before—it's odd. I watch him before I reply, "She's fine. She's upstairs sleeping still. I was going to wake her after I made breakfast. Would you like to see her now?" I ask.

The ball cap folds and unfolds—faster and faster.

"No, I—I came here to talk to you— to apologize, actually."

I frown.

He doesn't owe me an apology—it should be saved for his son.

The twirling stops, and he barrels on, "My son struggles to rely on people because of the father I have been to him. You've taken the brunt of his need to be independent, and for that, I'm sorry."

Kip's eyes don't stray from the ball cap in his hand, but as I watch him, I see tears brimming on the edges of his lashes.

Over the years, I've struggled with my feelings for him. I watched as he hurt my husband in a way that shaped our marriage, but I've also seen him as a grandfather. My little girl means the world to him. He changed for her, and he's tried to mend things with his son ever since. When I look at him now, there's defeat in the set of his shoulders, and I realize that maybe he hasn't forgiven himself.

"Kip, for many years growing up, I was angry at you on Brooks's behalf because I love him. I hated seeing him hurt. But—I watched you change when Avery was born. I don't think you need my forgiveness because I forgave you the moment you held my daughter three years ago." I stand and step forward to sit on the loveseat beside him, placing my hand on his trembling one before I continue. "I think maybe you need to forgive yourself. I will tell you like I told your son—you are worthy of love and forgiveness. You just have to let people close enough to show you."

Silent tears stream down his face, and my own cheeks are wet. His movements are slow and timid as he reaches up to wrap his arms around me, and I hold this broken man as he falls apart.

Sometimes, things have to fall apart to be put back together. It's what it took for my marriage, and I hope the same can be said for Kip and Brooks's relationship.

Kip's shoulders relax, and he pulls back to look at me again.

"Even if you've forgiven me, I want you to know I am sorry. I've talked with Brooks too, and—we're going to work on things."

I give him a watery smile and wipe the heel of my hand against my eyes.

"Thank you, Kip."

He nods, somber, and pulls something out of his pocket.

"I guess that only leaves one other reason I'm here." He shoves the envelope he pulled out towards me, and I take it with trembling fingers.

"What is this?" I ask.

The smirk from earlier is back when he answers, "One last letter from your husband. I'll be in the kitchen while you read it."

I don't notice him walking out of the room. I'm too focused on the letter. My hands shake as I rip open the envelope. When it finally opens, I slip out the paper and begin reading.

Emryn,

Meet me where it all began.

Love,

Brooks

Folding the letter, I run to the kitchen. Kip is leaning against the island with a goofy grin on his face.

"I'll watch Avery for you," he says without giving me a chance to ask.

I nod, calling a thank you over my shoulder as I rush upstairs to change.

————————————

When I pull into the school's back parking lot, the first thing that catches my eye is Brooks leaning against the fence, waiting for me. His smile is pure happiness.

I don't waste a minute getting out of the car, but my steps are slow and controlled when my feet hit the ground. My heart beats steadily as I approach the man I've loved since I was six.

Adoration and love shine through the blue of his eyes as he stares at me, and when I get close enough, he grabs my hand and pulls me behind him. I follow—flashes of the last time he dragged me behind him across the playground running through my mind.

It feels like a million years ago and just yesterday all at once. He glances back over his shoulder, and I swear I can see the boy he was twenty-two years ago. Then I blink, and that young boy is replaced with the man of my dreams.

We stop beside the fence, just like we did all those years ago, and I take a step towards him. When I'm inches away, the tips of our shoes touching, he holds his hand up to stop me.

"I have to get this out," he says. "I need to say everything I've been holding back—not in a letter—but to you."

My hands itch to touch him, so I grab the bottom of my sweatshirt to keep myself from reaching out. I want to hold him and share some of the strength I gained over the past few months, but I also can see his *need* to keep a little of his control.

"Emryn, I love you. I have since the day we stood here together twenty-two years ago. I never imagined where life would take us that day, but I don't regret any part of our journey. When I asked your dad if I could marry you, both times, he said yes with one stipulation—I had to protect your heart. I never dreamed that you might have to protect your heart from me, but that's what you did the day you left."

Swallowing hard, I reach my hand forward, letting my fingertips brush against his.

His ice-blue eyes hold mine, opening up all the struggles he's been holding back for so long.

"I don't regret you leaving that day," he continues. "It woke me up from the complacency that I fell into. I took you for granted. I've never had to leave my place of comfort because you've always been there. I've allowed myself to keep burying the parts of me that I didn't want to share, and in doing that, I hurt you. I don't want my past to change my future anymore. I trust you to shoulder my burdens with me—to love me in spite of me."

I can't hold back anymore. I take his hand in mine, but it isn't close enough. He pulls me into him until my head lays against his chest. My ear lies over his heart, and I listen as it beats in time with mine.

"Brooks—I messed up too. I should have paid closer attention to the things you weren't saying. I was too lost in my pain to see yours. When we got married, I promised to be there in good times and bad, but I didn't stand by that vow. We failed each other, but we've taken that failure and grown together."

His hand smooths over my back up to my hair, pulling gently at the ends and tilting my head up to him.

This man is the final piece of the puzzle of who I am. I'm a mom—a daughter, a student, and eventually a teacher—and, in all that, I am his.

My skin is on fire when his lips drop to my forehead, pressing a lingering kiss there. I close my eyes, and a smile flits across my lips as I savor the feeling of him. After a moment, he pulls back just enough to look at me again.

"I want to continue to grow with you until we are old and gray. I might still need time to process things in the future, but I promise I will communicate with you. I won't hide my broken pieces from you—even if another brother pops up."

A laugh—loud and abandoned—slips out. Brooks's smile widens—love and happiness.

"Surely, Kip can't have anymore. One surprise brother is enough for a lifetime."

"I wouldn't put it past the man," he says.

His smile drops just a bit, and I watch as he gets lost in his head. I hold my breath for a fraction of a second, waiting to see if he will share whatever is running through his mind.

"I hated being the only kid growing up, but in a way, I was glad no one else had to deal with the chaos of Kip. Now that I have a brother, does it make me selfish to want to bring him into the dysfunction?"

I put my hand over his heart, saying, "It doesn't make you selfish. You want to know your brother. That's not a crime."

Heat floods his cheeks as he reaches up and rubs the back of his neck. "I didn't make a great first impression with him."

"Maybe not," I say, "but you can make a better second—or third—or fourth impression. Life isn't just about one chance and one moment. You'll get your second chance with him."

"And what about you? Do I get a second chance with you?"

"I don't know," I say, pretending to think about it as I tap my finger against my chin.

"Maybe this will seal the deal," he says, sliding his hand into his pocket and pulling something out. He flips it over and opens his fingers, and there, lying in his palm is a Strawberry Ring Pop.

"That might do the trick, but I have some stipulations."

He never does let me tell him my stipulations this time, but I don't mind. I'm too busy kissing the man who will forever be my definition of love.

Epilogue

Brooks,

The definition of love is ever-changing—sometimes it's hard, an uphill struggle that we have to fight to get through, and sometimes it's sweet—like the first bite of ice cream on a warm day.

My definition has changed a lot over the years—gone through all the stages—but the one thing that remains the same is that they all include you, Avery, and this baby growing inside me.

We're having another baby. And even though I'm scared because I have one more year of school and Avery is about to start kindergarten, I know we have each other to make it through.

Love,
  Emryn

About the Author

T. Bell writes real and relatable romance novels with all of the swoon but none of the spice.

You can connect with me on:

☐ https://www.facebook.com/profile.php?id=100091232274801

🔗 https://www.tiktok.com/@authort.bell?_=8fvlXcapeBu&_r=1

🔗 https://instagram.com/authort.bell?igshid=YTQwZjQ0Nml0OA==

Also by T. Bell

Redemption

I'm a screw-up. Proof? On my first day back in town, I accidentally assaulted an officer, who also happens to be my brother's best friend... and the only man I've ever loved.

The thing is, that's only a blip on my record of mistakes. And believe me, the list is so long it could practically be two—one for all my usual screw-ups and the other for all my mistakes involving Hayes.

My tendency to make colossal mistakes around him is why I left town in the first place. He was like a jagged piece of glass pushing into all my open wounds. I needed time to heal.

Now I'm back, more broken than when I left, and clearly still making bad decisions.

The problem with being the screw-up is that someone is always bound to make you face your mistakes. My heart isn't ready for him to be the one who makes me face my demons, though, especially when he refuses to confront his own.

Letters of Faith
COMING SOON:
Grayson and Georgia's story.

Made in the USA
Monee, IL
10 September 2024

65381530R00138